J

UNDERLAND

ALSO BY

CHANDA HAHN

Underland Series

Underland
Underlord (*Coming 2017)*

Unfortunate Fairy Tale Series

UnEnchanted
Fairest
Fable
Reign
Forever

The Iron Butterfly Series

The Iron Butterfly
The Steele Wolf
The Silver Siren

UNDERLAND

Chanda Hahn

ISBN-10: 1522715665
ISBN-13: 978-1522715665
UNDERLAND

Cover design by Steve Hahn
Edited by Bethany Kaczmarek

www.chandahahn.com

To Bethany Kaczmarek
My editor & friend

When I was about to give up, you helped me create an even better story and fall in love with this book all over again.
Without you there wouldn't be an Underland.

One

Rain drizzled softly on the cardboard box, lulling the sleeping girl inside with a momentary sense of security. A can rattled along the cement and crashed into a brick wall. Kira's head snapped up, her startled heart pounding as she stared into the night, scanning for the source of the noise.

She wished for moonlight but saw only creeping steam rising from the sewer drains and crowding the alleyway. Shifting within the overturned appliance box, she pushed her sleeping bag off her shoulders to lean out of the box and gaze into the alley.

Madame Fortuna's neon sign buzzed and flickered, casting an eerie green glow on the steam, obscuring her vision even more. Kira waited and watched silently. Probably just a four-legged dumpster visitor, scavenging for food.

The aroma of baking bread told her it was pre-dawn, the only time of the day a pleasant smell competed with the rotten vestige of overflowing garbage. Kira's stomach grumbled in protest, but she was used the sound by now. And the numbness that followed.

When no other sign of movement came from the alley, she released the breath she'd been holding and inched backward into her box. She tugged her sleeping bag around her shoulders and listened to the sound of the light morning rain.

It was always drizzling in Portland. Most of the homeless learned to place their lean-tos, boxes, or shelters on top of a wooden pallet to separate themselves from the pooling water and to stretch a tarp over their shelter. Someone out there was benefitting from Kira's tarp even now. They'd stolen it just before nightfall, and she had very little hope of staying dry much longer. She'd have to find another box or tarp.

A shadow moved in front of her box's opening—bigger than any animal. Kira froze, her eyes narrowing as she reached into the small space behind her for the broken two-by-four she'd spiked with jagged nails. The shadow moved again, and a pair of big black boots stopped right in front of her box. Men's. Her mouth curled in a feral grin, and she pulled back the club to stab the ankles if the owner of the boots moved toward her.

She wasn't prepared for the assault to come through the top of the box. A second attacker's hands burst through the wet cardboard and gripped her neck. Strong arms pulled her against a solid chest, and a big hand covered her mouth with something foul-smelling. She kicked, fought, and scratched at the vise-like arms. But nothing helped. The arms lifted her high into the air, leaving her bag, club, and few possessions abandoned in her destroyed box as her assailant dragged her across the alley.

He smelled worse than her lecherous stepfather. She'd have to escape again. Good thing she'd had so much practice.

Hands removed a heavy grate from the sewer drain, and Kira screamed into the rag at the darkness below. The purple curtain in Madame Fortuna's storefront moved, and a pale, gaunt face appeared in the window, but the curtain quickly dropped back into place. Clearly, the old fortune teller wasn't interested in what lay beyond her fake crystal ball, heated flat, and big screen TV.

Or perhaps she'd already seen Kira's future. The woman had confronted her in the alley just the other day, her salt-and-pepper braid in much need of a thorough combing. Small gold rings made her plump fingers look like sausages as they'd poked seventeen-year-old Kira in the chest.

"Death!" Her voice rasped. "Death surrounds you."

"Go away, you hag!" Kira pushed her sausage finger away.

"Kira Lier," she chanted in a singsong voice. "Kira Lier brings death to us all." The woman had wandered back to the side door of her shop and hadn't come back out to bother Kira since. Now she wished she would.

She wished anyone would.

The sour gag in Kira's mouth turned her stomach. All she could make out around her were rough hands and darkness. They pushed her along tar-black passageways, the thinnest light slanting through each time they'd pass under a sewer grate—barely enough to illuminate the faces of her kidnappers, and even that for mere seconds. Two men.

One was tall with long brown hair pulled in a ponytail, the other short with dark skin and a bad buzz cut.

Both had an unbreakable grip on her forearms. She would sport bruises the next day, if she lived that long. But she wouldn't panic and start crying like most girls. She would wait and plot. If she struggled, she could blow her one chance of escape.

She didn't know where she was, other than underground. Her kidnappers obviously knew the sewers, knew where they were taking her. Right now, her best bet was to play the scared and compliant hostage. They might let their guard down.

"Dis one is quieter than the o'ers," the short one commented. He sounded almost disappointed.

"Alpo, do you miss the screaming? Just be glad this one isn't a biter. I hate when they bite."

"Oi just miss the begging. Oi like it when they beg for their life." As if trying to elicit a response from Kira, Alpo dug his nails into Kira's arms, hard.

Kira let out a whimper through her gag for him. She wouldn't fake tears, but it was time to pretend to be scared. Using her tongue, she pushed the gag out of her mouth and watched as it landed on her old worn army boot. She kept her head down to hide what she had done.

Alpo chuckled at Kira's whimpers. "Ya see, Vic, oi can still make them whimper."

Vic sighed, "Yes, and you'll get to hear plenty of screaming and begging when this one is taken to the pens. Don't worry none."

There was less light as Alpo and Vic pulled Kira farther into the tunnels and away from the sewer grates. Rank smelling fluid leaked in through the soles of her boots, cold and wet. She ignored the odor and cold as she counted steps and turns, hoping to retrace her route out.

She didn't doubt that she would escape.

They stopped at a dead end. Kira looked up, puzzled. Alpo let go of her arm and stood in front of a huge cement block covered with bad graffiti and the word *Monsters*, outlined in neon pink. She had to stop herself from snorting in amusement at the bad artwork.

Alpo walked over to the side of the brick wall and dug his fingers into the cracks and pulled.

She wasn't sure what she was expecting, but watching a five-foot-nine man move a two-foot thick brick wall with his bare hands was not on her list. It wasn't humanly possible. Maybe it was a faux wall, a movie prop used to camouflage the entrance. Or maybe there was a lever and hidden lock used to swing the massive door. A dark passageway opened up behind the wall, and a stagnant smell blew from the darkness. The hair on Kira's arms stood.

They hadn't blindfolded her, so they clearly believed this was going to be a one-way trip. And if they dragged her in there and closed the wall she probably would be trapped. There was no chance she could move that wall on her own. And only one person held onto her arm for the moment.

Kira planted her feet and pulled as hard as she could away from Vic. When he gripped tighter and yanked her towards him, she used the momentum to throw a left-handed punch.

Vic yelled and dropped her arm to grab his bloodied nose. It was a shame Kira had to use her weak arm. She'd aimed to break his nose.

Kira sprinted in the direction they had come, praying she could remember the turns correctly. Adrenaline made her legs fly beneath her. It was harder to reverse the directions under pressure, but she refused to look back, to give in to the voice that was screaming in her ear, *Turn around. Look.*

Vic was screaming at Alpo behind her, and their longer legs were quickly catching up to her. She ran, turned left, turned right. *Did I pass that lump of garbage already?*

Left.

Fear flooded her.

Dead end.

Breathing hard, she spun to correct her mistake.

Too late. Arms like iron encased her. Alpo grunted into her ear and tried to squeeze the breath out of her.

Kira kicked. She bit. She squirmed, used every technique her Navy SEAL father had taught her. She wasn't going down without a fight. She wouldn't betray his memory that way.

She'd never quit trying like her mother had.

Vic came up behind Alpo, wiping the blood from his nose on his sleeve. "Well, you have definitely made this interesting."

His viper-like grin ticked Kira off. She spit in his face.

Vic's grin turned ugly. His eyes darkened, and his hands clenched her throat.

No air. Between Alpo compressing her chest and Vic strangling her, she was losing consciousness fast. Her father's smiling face flashed in front of her.

I'm sorry, Dad.

TWO

Ears ringing and throat raw, Kira blinked and tried to make sense of what she saw and felt.

Getting past the rancid smell took a little effort, but she could piece some details together. A lantern hung from a pole in front of them and cast an eerie glow over the cavern. She wasn't walking, and the men weren't carrying her. Just a gentle bobbing motion. A bench seat pressed into her cheek, but there was no vehicle ceiling. Her hands were zip-tied behind her back, her feet bound with a worn black belt. The crick in her neck told her she had been lying in this awkward position for quite a while.

The bobbing was gentle, rhythmic.

They must be in a boat.

The skiff, or what she could see of it, was a combination of hodge-podge materials and shoddy work. Numerous coats of paint—some fresh, some older and half-chipped—covered the metal siding. A can filled with dead fish sat by the bow. The source of the stench. Blowflies fluttered around the disgusting fish in their different stages of decomposition.

Kira held her breath and only moved her eyes to see who was in the skiff. She counted six feet—two in green boots, probably Vic's; two in sneakers, she bet they were Alpo's; and the other pair of boots belonged to someone new.

She tilted her head a bit and saw what looked like green-hued water beneath them. *Too much effort.* Easing her head back into its awkward resting position, she waited for the ringing in her ears to stop.

Faint conversation drifted her direction.

"What do you plan to do with this one?" the newcomer asked.

"Sell it of course," Alpo grunted. "Grater is still paying plenty of money for slaves."

"I don't think he would pay much for it. This one looks pretty weak. You know he likes fighters."

"It mighta been a bit of a fighter if Vic 'adn't choked the life near out of it." Alpo snickered.

Kira desperately wished she could see the new guy's face. His questions were finally giving her information she could use to her advantage.

"Well then, we sell it as feeder for a vamp or zeke," Vic spat out. He kicked Kira, and she slumped sideways falling on her back.

Kira grunted. She finally had a view of the speaker, but a long weathered hood covered his face. She could only see his pale hands.

"It's human! You brought a human down here. How dare you go against the ban from scavenging the surface world? The penalty is a month in lockup or worse—the games."

"Eh, what Grater doesn't know won't hurt him or the price none, if you keep quiet." Alpo stood up and the skiff rocked back and forth. "You don't plan on making trouble do you?" He cracked his knuckles threateningly.

The hooded cloak swerved Kira's way and then looked out over the river of sewage they were floating on. "No. I could get in trouble just by association. Risk your necks, not mine."

They were quiet, and only the occasional sound of an oar correcting their course interrupted the silence. Lights flickered across the cavern ceiling as they picked up speed. The skiff skimmed the water smoothly until something large knocked against the bottom of the boat.

Vic, his face twisted in worry, reached for the bucket of dead fish. She heard the knocking again, and something bulky slammed into the boat. It swayed and tilted, letting sewage spill over the side into the bottom. Kira lifted her feet to avoid the reeking water that ran towards her body, but she couldn't avoid it. Cold soaked into her clothes, and she gagged at the smell that now permeated her khaki pants and t-shirt.

"Dang it, Vic. Are you going to toss in the chum, or are you waiting for the thing to ask you on a date first?" The cloaked man snatched the pail and tossed the dead fish into the green depths.

The knocking stopped, followed by a splash and a deep bellow from beneath the water.

Alpo peered over the edge of the boat, searching the water for movement. "Is it gone?"

Vic, visibly shaken, wiped his sweaty brow with a rag. "I don't think I will ever get used to the city's new gatekeeper. I think I preferred Horace."

"No, thank you. It is way easier to acquire dead fish than wrangling live cats for Horace."

Alpo looked over the water and shrugged. "But why does she have to get so orn'ry?"

Vic stood straighter. "Yeah, Nessie's been PMSing ever since somebody spotted her in Scotland and the gods demoted her. She's the only one desperate enough to take the job," he laughed cruelly.

The cloaked man leaned back and stared Alpo down. "She takes her job to protect the city seriously, unlike some. Don't pay the toll, and you'll learn what it's like to be fish food."

A humongous gray tail rose thirty feet out of the water and came crashing down next to the skiff, missing Vic by inches. The boat rose, almost capsized from the weight of the cresting swell. Sewage water soaked all four passengers. The sound of a groaning submarine under pressure rose from the depths—Nessie's laughter.

The immense tail made Kira wonder about the sea monster's actual proportions. Had she really heard them right? What in the world was the Loch Ness Monster doing living in the sewers of Portland?

Were they even in the metro area anymore? The cloaked man looked towards Kira, and she glared heat his way.

He was the first to drop eye contact. She smirked.

"Do you have a name?" He asked her.

She simply stared in return.

"Not a talkative one, are you?"

Kira turned to study the glittering cavern. The skiff had entered an enormous chamber with more torchlight than she'd seen before. Here, what she'd thought was a reflection from the water really seemed to be sparkling diamonds, rubies, and emeralds. The torchlight made the gems dance and sparkle. Her eyes widened in disbelief.

"It's pretty isn't it?" The man spoke. "There's more diamonds in our walls than in all of Africa. It won't do anyone any good though. It's cursed—the price we pay for anonymity. If mortals make it past Nessie, they lose all thought of searching deeper when they see the jewels." Kira believed him, because she found it almost painful to pull her gaze away from the diamonds.

She closed her eyes and looked away but found it hard to breathe; she gasped and felt herself begin to shake. It was as if she was addicted after only one glance and was suddenly in withdrawal, worse than any heroin or meth addict.

Alpo swore. "Forgot to cover its eyes. It ain't gonna catch us a good price if we don't do something quick."

Kira's body began convulsing, and her tongue felt twenty times larger than her mouth.

Vic searched his pockets but came up empty. "I don't got any. I wasn't expecting it to be awake already."

Kira couldn't believe it. She was going to die for looking at a stupid wall covered in diamonds. Just when she felt as if her heart was going to explode, something warm and soft touched her tongue. Chocolate. As soon as the sweet flavor reached her taste buds, her body relaxed.

"Chocolate is the only cure for madness," the man said. As he held her in his arms and leaned over her body, she could see the bottom of his chin. Maybe it was because she was still drugged with greed, but Kira really liked that chin. There was something hard and soft about it at the same time—it even had a dimple in it. *My cousin would call that a butt-chin.* The thought made her chuckle.

Alarmed, the man dropped her, and her head hit the bench with a thud.

"Ow! That hurt!" Those were the first words Kira had spoken to her kidnappers—not her ideal choice for a starter conversation. She would have preferred a slew of words that would make her grandma cringe. But at this moment, Kira didn't have full control of her faculties. The whole thing was pretty hilarious, really. She giggled harder and then laughed loudly.

"It's insane!" Alpo cried.

"No, she's drunk. It's a possible side effect from the chocolate and the high. It only happens to humans—if the person hasn't eaten in a while." Kira felt the man look her over again as if judging her. "By the way, Vic. You owe me thirty freedom tokens for that chocolate."

"What! That's absurd. It's sewer-way robbery!"

"Thirty. Because I saved her life, and you wouldn't have made one freedom token if she was crazy. The zekes don't like to eat crazies, tends to make them unpredictable." He was the only one who referred to her as a person.

Vic looked at something metal on his wrist and grimaced. "Uh, I'll have to pay you back as soon as we sell it."

Kira bit her lip to keep anymore stupid giggles from escaping her lips. She would not make a fool of herself. When she felt she had finally regained command and her composure, she turned toward where the boat was taking them—and almost lost it again.

An underground city. Alit with various Christmas lights, neon, and what looked to be some old restaurant signs. *It must stretch for miles.* Kira saw skyscrapers, oddly-shaped buildings, stores all made from rusted, recycled metals and stone.

It was hideously beautiful.

The boat slowed as Alpo maneuvered it towards the dock. The man with the cape jumped out first and secured the tether. When Vic got out, he hauled Kira up after him, but her legs were weak and still bound, and she crashed to the wooden dock. Vic leaned down, unstrapped the belt from her ankles, and demanded she walk.

She got her bearings and watched as the man that had no name gave her one last long look before turning his back and disappearing among the throng of people.

She turned to take in the mass of passersby. No one even considered lending a hand. A large man, probably the harbormaster, came over to speak with Vic. His leathery skin stretched tightly over his odd and otherworldly face. He stopped, staring at her with jaundiced yellow eyes, and then opened his mouth and hissed at her.

She jumped back in surprise, but managed to shoot him an irritated look.

But then it hit her. She studied the harbormaster, looked at the nearest passerby, and realized just what the oddity was. She swallowed and tried to take a step back toward the boat, back to a semblance of safety.

The few sparse feet of dock was the only thing that separated her from a city full of monsters.

Three

Kira wasn't sure which oddity truly awakened her to her non-human counterparts first. It could have been the ten-foot troll selling hotdogs, or what she hoped were hotdogs—the toppings looked questionable and nothing like relish. Or maybe it was the manticore pushing a baby carriage full of kittens.

Kira stood frozen. Alpo had to physically lift her and drag her into the city. Maybe she had hit her head harder than she thought. Maybe she was just delusional.

But the farther they walked, the more complex her dream became. There was a small dragon wearing a cap and selling newspapers. A half-man, half-bear was leaning against a dented taxi, waiting for a patron. Did his fares ever ask to go to the surface? There were werewolves, trolls, ogres, and even a few that looked human, like Vic and Alpo. But Kira had to wonder if that was just a ruse. This city didn't cater to the human kind. The multifaceted monster city thriving under Portland filled her with so many unanswered questions that Kira completely forgot about escape.

She lost her chance when Vic and Alpo took her to Grater, a five-foot rat with long yellowed teeth that jutted over his bottom lip, who immediately started pawing her body in examination.

Her first response was to freeze at the hand reaching for her, but then she shook off her creepy memories and fought. Kira threw her head back and head butted Alpo, who held her from behind.

"Oi, that 'urt," he grunted and his fingers dug into her arms.

Kira twisted her body and used Alpo to kick the giant rat. He backed off, but not before she spat at him. She had to assume he was the one who was going to buy her, and she wanted to deter him by being as disgusting as she could.

She examined him at the same time. One large round ear was torn, and his tail had seen better days—no tip. The rat wore clothes that looked to have come out of a garbage bin. Kira could respect that because she shopped dumpsters herself.

Grater walked around Kira, his long nose brushing against her shoulder and sniffing her hair. "This one smells of the surface. What slave farm did you say you got it from?"

Vic rolled his shoulders and smiled. "My Uncle's in San Fran. I had to travel a ways to bring it, and our home tunnel was blocked so we had to take a detour through the surface. But you can tell by looking at it, it's from down here." He sounded like a used car salesman.

"He's lying." Kira glared at Vic and Alpo.

Vic's eyes went wide in pretend shock. "How can you say such a thing? We've taken such good care of you." He turned his back and addressed Grater. "That's what we get for getting too attached to them. You start giving them privileges, feed them, and sooner or later, they turn on you." He paused and looked at Kira sadly. He reached into his pocket and pulled out what she presumed was forged paperwork, with her fake identity on it.

"I've never seen you before in my life. You kidnapped me from outside the Pearl District. I don't know you." Kira wasn't sure what good trying to prove her humanity would do, but she obviously didn't belong down here.

Alpo came up behind her and smacked her on the head. "Quiet, slave, or we'll take you back to the farm."

Grater watched the exchange through narrowed eyes. He scanned the paperwork and asked to see her brand. She grinned; she knew she didn't have any kind of mark on her body that would give truth to their lie.

Vic smiled. "Gladly! Alpo, hold it down."

Hands gripped Kira's hair and pulled her head down across the vendor table. They smashed her face against rotted fruit and what she assumed was some kind of dead squirrel. The stench filled her nostrils and she had to close her eyes, breathe through her mouth to keep from vomiting. Clawed fingers moved against her neck, and she tried to buck backwards in defense. The rat traced a mark behind her ear, and she winced in pain. Something was wrong.

"Well, everything does seem to be in order, even if its slave mark looks a little newer than the others." Grater squinted and looked between Alpo and Vic thoughtfully. "Where's its bracer?" He pointed a gnarled finger at her wrist.

"Malfunctioned. We're waiting to register it to get a new one."

As soon as they let her, Kira straightened up and tried to look for a reflective surface. She found one in a polished broken mirror a few feet away and had to crane her neck to see the almost indistinguishable hash mark tattooed below her right ear. Her skin was slightly pink where the ink had been applied, but it looked days old. If they'd tattooed her when she was knocked out, she could have been unconscious for days, not hours.

How far had they traveled since then? She'd never find her way home now.

"I'll give you three hundred," Grater intoned nonchalantly.

"I won't accept anything less than five," Vic argued.

"It looks a little wild in the eyes. I can't feed it to the zekes like that." Grater turned as if to leave.

"Nonsense, it's stubborn, not crazy. Four fifty." Vic looked furious, veins bulging on his forehead. Alpo stood quietly behind Vic and held onto Kira, but he kept shifting on the balls of his feet.

"It is too thin, not enough meat on the bones. I would have to fatten it up to use it as feed, and that costs me more money. I'll give you two fifty."

"Wait, you're supposed to go up, not down!" Vic screeched and grabbed at his hair. "Fine. Three hundred, and use it however you want." Negotiations were obviously not his strong suit.

"Deal. Three hundred freedom tokens." Grater smiled evilly at getting his first price. Or it could have been happily. It was hard to tell with his snout and whiskers. He pulled up his sleeve to reveal a metal arm band with a black digital screen and keypad. He tapped it, then held out his arm. The screen flashed with a lots of slashes and circles—like something you might see on an ancient artifact.

Vic revealed his own bracer and touched it to Grater's. A low chime sounded and green digital marks on Vic's changed to include Grater's money.

Grater disappeared into a stall and reappeared moments later with a larger metal band attached to a chain. Kira struggled against Alpo's strength. The death-grip he had on her head said he was definitely not human. Grater lifted the collar up to her neck, and when the metal lock clicked, Kira fought the urge to scream and claw at the band around her neck.

She was proud that she didn't break down and cry. Grater tugged on her new leash, and Kira yanked back angrily. In a wink, Grater flipped the chain around Kira's legs and pulled, knocking her onto her back hard. Blinding pain shot through her vision. *Man was the rat fast.*

Grater put one foot on her chest and leaned his foul smelling snout towards her face. "Don't give me trouble." He stepped back and allowed her room to get up. He picked up a walking stick and beckoned her to follow him. Another rat came out from the back and took over the vendor stall. Grater cut through an alley and headed towards what looked to be the downtown area.

"They were lying to you," Kira spoke heatedly. "You were dumb enough to believe them."

Grater picked up his stick and whacked Kira on the back of the head. "Slaves don't talk!" He walked in silence for a few beats. "I wasn't dumb enough to believe them. Vic's Uncle's farm hasn't had any slaves in years. The slave farms are dying, especially with the ban against going to the surface. But we're the ones going extinct. While your kind multiply like cockroaches on the surface, we are left here to rot in the underbelly of society. Forgotten, the biggest crime of all." Grater spit into the street. "But you're in our world now."

"If you knew they were lying and I was from the surface, why did you buy me?" This time she was prepared. When the stick came her way, she ducked, and she would have cheered except that she missed the return swing aimed at her shins. She buckled to the ground in pain.

"You might as well get adjusted to our way of doing things down here. Doesn't matter where you're from, whether the borderlands or the surface. You'll still be fodder, and even fodder has a price. But I'm warning you, any funny business and I'll kill you right here."

Kira pitched forward, pressed her head to the littered sidewalk, and tried to flex her purple fingers. She had lost all feeling in her hands; the zip tie had cut off most circulation. "Give me a second."

Grater didn't swing at her for talking.

But he did pull out a knife.

The blade arced towards her back, and Kira sucked in her breath.

A quick snap, and her hands were freed. They flopped uselessly to her side, and she took a moment to stare at the purple and gray lumps that were her hands.

Fear for her life out of the way momentarily, Kira panicked over her useless hands. Pain like a searing flame licked her skin. Kira tried to move her fingers, but she still couldn't.

Grater grabbed her hands and brought them up to his nose and inhaled the scent of her palms.

"Not dead yet. Dying, but it can be reversed. It doesn't change your value any if you don't have hands. Some might prefer it." He yanked on her chain, and Kira lurched forward, trying to get to her feet. Not easy without the support of her hands.

Kira followed Grater, rubbing her hands along her thighs, forcing blood back into them. They still looked grayish, but the purple was fading.

Grater ducked into an alley and stopped before a large metal door. After a series of quick raps, the door opened. A giant with a missing eye escorted them into a large courtyard filled with cages. He opened an empty cage and waited for Grater to take Kira's lead chain off. But first, Grater attached a band to her wrist, similar to the ones she'd seen almost everyone wearing. Then, with a quick kick, Grater sent Kira flailing to the dirt floor.

Her arms too weak to catch her body weight, she struggled to get up. Before she could get to the door, the giant slammed it in her face and turned the key. He gave her a grin when she flung herself against the bars in anger.

"You no good, flea-bitten, dirty son of a…" She didn't finish because he opened his mouth and let out a deafening roar. The stench from his toxic breath made Kira gag. She turned to search for fresher air and sat down against the side of her cage. She glared at the giant.

Grater ignored her, speaking to his partner, a human-sized Doberman in brown breeches and a red leather vest. They both gave her speculative looks before walking towards the far side of the courtyard.

She spent twenty minutes prying at the metal band, banging it, trying to remove the thing from her wrist. All she did was give herself painful red scratches up and down.

She couldn't handle looking at the digital green lights. But she soon noticed that if she didn't touch it, they would fade to black.

Kira lifted her head to watch Grater leaning against a wall lined with metal slats—a whole *series* of cages.

"You're a human aren't you?" a hushed voice whispered.

Kira's neck snapped in the direction of the speaker, a tall girl with brown skin and dark green hair. She wore the tattered remains of what looked like a dress made from leaves and moss. Was there someone in every one of the cages? How many prisoners did they keep here?

"Yeah, you smell human. Which means you'll be dead soon," the girl continued.

"I'm alive now, and that's what matters." Kira's voice lacked the haughtiness she'd had earlier. Here was a young girl in her own situation who knew more than she did. She needed whatever information the girl could give her if she was going to survive.

"They are going to sell you," she gestured to the other cages around the courtyard, "to the highest bidder. And with you being human, that means only one thing. Death."

"That's what everyone keeps telling me. But I'm still alive."

"For now."

"What's your name?" Kira asked.

"Sable."

"I'm Kira." She waited a second and then asked. "So what is this, and how do I get it off?"

Sable sunk back into her cage, and it took a moment before she answered.

"You're not from a farm." She looked scared. "Otherwise you'd know that already. Who are you?"

"I'm from above," Kira pointed up with one finger. "Portland."

She shook her head and started to rock back and forth in her cage. "Oh no no no, then you'll definitely never be allowed to go home…alive."

Kira waited patiently for the girl to come to her senses. She held up her wrist and waited for Sable to reply.

She spoke softly. Sadly. "It's your bracer. You've been registered as an Underlander. Your tracker, your identity—it's all tied into that little machine, and it won't come off, unless you…" She made sawing motion across her wrist.

Kira paled at the thought.

"But even if you do, they'll find you and attach a bigger one to your neck." Sable pointed to another cage where the inhabitant was missing a hand. A much more permanent metal collar surrounded his neck.

"That's horrible." Kira shivered and eyed the band. Maybe she could leave it for the time being. "What is this place?" Kira let the questions spill. "And how do I get out of here?"

Sable paused and looked around. "This is the Gamblers' Market. Plutus calls in gambling debts, and debtors are forced to come here and try and sell their services. If a family member can, they'll come and pay off the debt. But if no one buys a debtor, then they may be bought by a sponsor and forced to compete in the games anyway."

"Games?"

Her green cheeks turned brown when she blushed. "Games, gauntlets, challenges. They're all the same. Our whole economy—our whole society—revolves around the games. Working for the games, training fighters for the games, competing for the games, betting and losing on the games."

"That sounds kind of absurd."

"Does it?" Sable flipped her green tresses over her shoulder and sighed. "I hear your world spends billions, and cities revolve around basketball, baseball, and feetball."

"Football."

"Football, yes. We don't have that, but why is it so hard to imagine we're any different? We have the ever-changing games. By decree of the Underlords of Olympus Tower. If you compete and win, both you and your sponsor—or owner—make tons of freedom tokens. But you're a *human*," she emphasized the word dramatically. "So Raz will end up selling you to feed a sponsor's vamp or zeke or anything else with a taste for your kind."

"Zeke?"

Kira's blank stare made Sable sigh like a petulant child. "A zeke is a zombie. They *feed* on humans, you know. Well actually they feed on anyone, but they prefer humans.

Kira's smile fell. There really wasn't an easy way out of here. She'd spotted a few huge looking beasts, dragon, a Cyclops, and what looked to be about five other humans, but Kira knew better than to assume they were like her. She was most surprised at the quiet nature of the young teen in the cage to Kira's right. He sat on the floor, head bowed, with his elbows resting on his knees. He didn't look scared or frightened about his predicament. He seemed casually resigned, and he ignored Kira completely.

Raz and Grater finished their conversation and then walked around to each of the cages and spoke quietly. When they paused in front of Sable's cage, Kira strained to overhear what they said.

"What about this one? What should I put on the bill about this one?" Raz, the intimidating Doberman asked, his voice a deep growl.

Grater crooked one long finger at Sable. "Swamp Nymph: strengths include cunning, speed, resourcefulness, and ability to maneuver through water and woods with ease. Weaknesses: physical strength and fear of fire." Sable looked terrified.

They moved to Kira's cage. Raz took a quick sniff. "She smells human."

Grater nodded. "Yes, I think Remus or Selene would buy this one as food. I heard Creeper one just won another race. I should bet on him next time."

"We have a conundrum with this one." They moved to the boy's cage on the right.

Grater went on to explain about the young man, but Kira didn't hear what they said. Her mind finally began to give into fear. That Madame Fortuna was right. Her death was imminent.

Raz and Grater moved on.

Kira looked up when she felt the hairs on the back of her neck rise. Who was watching her? Her eyes met the boy's. He still hadn't moved but he was now staring at her, interested. Dark hair flowed over his forehead, and his eyes seemed to burn with a fire deep inside. His gaze made Kira shift uncomfortably.

It usually took a lot to make Kira nervous. He was looking at her longingly, almost like a lover would. He wasn't blinking and he wasn't turning away. Kira tried to stare him down. Slowly, oh, so slowly, the corner of his mouth rose, just a millimeter in the hint of a smile. But this was not a smile to lift her spirits.

This smile chilled Kira to the bone.

"Sable!" Kira whispered over her shoulder.

"What?" she called back with a bored tone.

"What is he? Why is he staring at me like that?" Kira continued to whisper in hopes that the guy in the cage next to her wouldn't overhear.

"Isn't it obvious?" She waited, savoring the moment. "That's a zeke. You're dinner."

Four

The slave courtyard was dark and all of the slaves slept, except for the boy in the cage next to her who kept casting hungry looks her way. The same look her stepfather always had. The only light came from the one neon cigarette sign that was left on, which cast a lavender halo on the courtyard wall. The color and glow reminded her of her unicorn nightlight—the one her daddy had given her—and it helped dispel the fear.

She missed him dearly, missed the sound of his voice, and even now wished he was by her side, chasing away the nightmares. Because in her child mind, darkness meant sleep, sleep meant nightmares, and nightmares meant…monsters.

Her late father, Philip, was great at comforting her. He had advice about everything, even if he was usually quoting someone famous. His favorite quote was the one he always used to calm her. "Sweetheart, there's nothing to fear but fear itself."

"But how do I get my fear to not be afraid?" she had childishly replied.

He'd smiled, pulled out that purple unicorn nightlight, and plugged it into the wall. Then he kissed her forehead and whispered, "Darkness cannot drive out darkness; only light can do that." From that night on, she'd never had another nightmare, until one walked into her home seven years later in the guise of her stepfather.

Her father, Philip Lier, had just become a Navy SEAL when he met her mom, the love of his life. Their whirlwind romance led to a quick wedding, but Philip and Ellie had the kind of forever love that made the neighbors jealous. Philip hoped for lots of strapping boys to follow in his military footsteps, but they had only Kira. Her mom had almost died during labor, and the news that they shouldn't expect baby Kira to live more than a few days devastated her. Then they added that she couldn't have any more children. And she gave up.

But from hour one, Kira had been a Daddy's little fighter. She spent the first few months of her life in the ICU where he doted on his baby girl, even if he never got to hold her except when wearing gloves.

Her mom on the other hand? Just wallowed in I-Disappointed-My-Husband Land. And nothing Kira's dad could do could convince her he was still happy with their family.

When Philip Lier died a hero, nothing mattered to her mom but numbing her pain. Not even Kira.

Why was Kira thinking about all of this now? She never reminisced about her childhood—except her father. She'd left her mother, her horrible stepfather, and her past behind her. Two long years ago. Now she was faced with a different kind of monster.

Kira quickly wiped away the wetness that began to form in the corner of her eyes. She would not feel sorry for herself.

Instead, she'd figure out how the people here knew day from night. She looked around the courtyard. Without a sun or moon, she could only tell it was nighttime because the city became quieter and fewer signs were left on. Darkness was always there, waiting to creep in, and she shivered at the thought of what would happen if every light in the city went out. She would be surrounded in pitch black by hungry monsters. Did they get power outages?

A scream came from outside the courtyard walls, followed by low growls, and chomping noises. She shuddered. Something or someone was being eaten. This only confirmed her worst fear.

The giant guard awoke and came running out of a side building with a large club. He scanned the inhabitants of the cells, moved towards the large iron doors, and waited, club at the ready. His eye searched the twenty-foot wall for movement. When the sounds of chomping and devouring ceased beyond the wall and no more noise came, the giant stalked back to the building.

Kira couldn't let it go so easily; the hair on the back of her arms still stood on end.

Stop it! she told herself. She would get through this. Well, maybe she would if the zeke in the cage next to her ever slept. It didn't seem like he needed to, and he had been staring at her for the last twelve hours. It was enough to drive anyone insane.

She didn't want to sleep with her back to him, but facing him was just as creepy. She sat in the corner of the cage and stared at the ground. What seemed like hours later, the hustle and bustle of activity of the waking town dispelled the quietness. But to her bodily clock, the hours seemed wrong. It felt like they slept during the human day and were active at night. It made sense—that's how they caught her when she was trying to sleep.

Movement by the gate made her glance up. The giant had opened the door to allow people inside. Grater stood to his right with a clipboard. Each entrant transferred money to him before entering. At least twenty bidders had come in, but she thought she'd counted only fifteen slaves to choose from. Kira would have been nervous if she wasn't so curious.

These buyers were obviously from a different class than the people on the street. No dumpster wardrobes here. The clothes looked finely tailored to fit their needs, from large to small tails.

Again, most looked human until one of them smiled. Kira saw the hint of fangs. A rail-thin woman, almost translucent in skin color, pushed her long, black hair over her shoulder and stared into a cage. One buyer was a large white rabbit, another was half-man, half-snake.

Sable was getting excited despite her grim outlook of being sold. She recognized all the buyers, all trainers for the games. If Sable was lucky, she could earn her freedom. "The half-snake is Ssirone. He is a Paladin, a champion that has earned his freedom. Now he owns his own gym and trains some of the strongest and deadliest fighters."

"What about the rabbit?" Kira asked. Surely a rabbit wouldn't feed her to a monster.

Sable actually shuddered. "Don't catch his eye," she whispered. "He tends to starve and beat his fighters, and most die before ever getting the chance to compete." Kira ducked her head quickly.

Each buyer went to every cage and poked and prodded the slaves inside, assessing their value and abilities as if they were prized horses. Sable tried to stand and look proud in her cage, but Kira could see the girl visibly shaking. The vampire looked interested in buying Sable, but so did Ssirone. The boy zeke gathered a huge crowd of interested buyers.

Only the rabbit and a snake man paid Kira any attention—both said the same thing when they looked at her.

"Hmm, human. This would make a good treat." The rabbit rubbed his white chin thoughtfully.

"Not if I buy her for my champion first," Ssirone joked.

The rabbit looked at Ssirone with contempt in his eyes. A knot began to turn in Kira's stomach. So these were sponsors.

"Now, now, Cottontail, don't get your scruff in a rut. If you want the human, then you bid for it," Ssirone challenged, pointing to his bracer.

"Maybe I will, you moron. And don't call me Cottontail. My name is Peter, just Peter."

Kira almost snickered aloud when she heard the rabbit's name, but her quick intake of breath made Peter's black beady eyes jump to her. Her stomach chose that moment to growl loudly with hunger. Peter threw his head back and laughed in high-pitched staccato bursts.

Raz let the buyers mingle about the courtyard for an hour before he barked loudly that they were about to begin the bidding. Kira saw Grater watching the proceedings from a distance. Raz brought out the first slave with his chain and made him stand on a metal stage constructed of oil drums and planks of wood.

The slave was young, with sandy hair and oversized eyes. He looked slightly ill until his long tongue slipped out of his mouth and snagged a large horsefly out of the air. In one second, the fly was gone, and Kira was the one left looking ill. Apparently that didn't impress any of the buyers, because no one bought him. *Huh.* She thought they were all getting sold.

Maybe she had misunderstood. Maybe if no one bought her they would let her go.

Two more slaves went without a single bid before a tall muscular boy was led up to the stage. There were a few whispers and comments when the boy just stood there.

Raz angrily took out a Taser and shocked the slave into compliance. As the boy leaned back and howled in pain, his body grew, and his face elongated into a wolf. Fur appeared on his arms and legs, and his muscles ripped through his pants. He stood there panting, his tongue hanging out like an overworked dog's.

A bidding war began for the young werewolf. He sold for an exorbitant amount to his archenemy the vampire.

Sable was unlucky as well, for she sold fairly quickly to Ssirone the snake. Her natural athleticism and speed would aid her, if she survived the training and became a fighter. According to Sable, the training was almost as gruesome and difficult as actually competing in the events.

Kira was surprised when the zeke boy walked up to the stage freely, with no chains, and dared his captors to bid on him with his hate-filled eyes. And bid they did. He went for double the amount of the werewolf, to a tall man in the back of the room.

When all of the non-human slaves had a chance to be bid on, and the ones that were bought were taken to a different holding pen, she thought it was over.

It wasn't. Large ogres moved the stage, and the buyers backed up to the walls. An overturned garbage can sat in the middle of the courtyard with a silver knife resting on the bottom, waiting. Kira wished Sable was still in the pen next to her so she could ask what was going on, but she had to wait. Frustrated.

Grater stepped forward and pointed to two of the cages with unsold slaves—the one with the frog boy and a boy with skin like slime. Two men stood by the cages and waited for Grater's mark to open them. The boys inside the cages moved towards the door, waiting to pounce. Grater whistled.

The men threw open the doors.

Slime boy and frog boy shot out of their cages for the trashcan and the knife. Slime boy was faster and had almost reached the knife when the frog boy shot out his tongue and snatched it from the top of the can. The first boy, as soon as he saw that frog boy had the knife, jerked out of his reach, fell backwards, and turned to run.

Escape was impossible. The only exit was blocked. Kira was confused by the loud cheering from the bystanders.

Frog boy took the knife out of his mouth and stalked his prey. He leapt into the air and came down on slime boy's back, feet first, knife second. The boy twitched once, twice, and then died.

Kira turned and started to gag. She fell to her knees and reached for a tin of water to splash her face. Had she really witnessed one slave kill another? Looking up, she saw the frog boy dance in glee. Raz took his hand and held it up in the air in victory, which began the bidding all over again. Frog boy sold for almost as much as the werewolf.

So, if no one would bid on you, you were either sent to the games or you were allowed to battle it out, kill your opponent in a slave match. You could prove your worth and get a sponsor to buy you. Well, if the choice was kill or be killed running, she wanted to run.

But her confidence at escaping was slipping every hour.

After two more death matches and two more slaves getting sold off, Raz drew the crowd's attention to Kira. Her heart thudded loudly. Her hands balled into fists as she listened to the murmur of the crowd die off to be replaced by a few hisses of disgust. Others laughed in her direction. Would she even make it to the block or would they maul her?

The giant with toxic breath opened her cage and grabbed Kira around the throat, forcing the collar to bite painfully into her neck. She clawed at his wrists as he dragged her out of her cage. They didn't even bother putting her on the stage, just dumped her on the ground in the middle of the monsters. Her chain landed near Grater.

Raz's voice rang out loudly, "And over here we have a human fresh from the borderlands. Yours to do with as you please. Kill it, torture it, or eat it. Let the bid begin at five hundred freedom tokens."

Kira jumped up and spit at Raz. She would have lunged for him, but Grater had a hold of the chain around her collar and yanked her back to the ground. Her attitude made some of the buyers nervous, and they physically backed away showing their unwillingness to bid.

"What, you don't like a little bit of spirit?" Grater called out.

Kira saw the small victory she'd gained and decided to play the wild and unstable card. Hoping to intimidate others into backing off, she paced. Careful to stay within the boundaries of her leash, she stared down the bidders. With the smaller ones, she squared off to face them, head high. She even feinted in their direction.

"Five hundred," Ssirone called out, unfazed by her aggressiveness.

"Six," Peter held up his arm.

"Seven" Ssirone turned to glare at the rabbit, his head swaying side to side like a cobra. Peter's gaze locked with Ssirone's and his ears dropped. His nose twitched once then froze—hypnotized by the snake man's gaze.

It was impossible even for Kira to tear her eyes away from Ssirone. She could feel the fear running through her blood in the rhythm of her heartbeat. Without even making eye contact with him, she could feel the effects of his predatory stare. Peter on the other hand, didn't seem to be as aware as she was.

"Seven hundred, going once," Raz called out. "Going twice."

Kira swallowed and saw the corner of Ssirone's mouth lift in excitement. He knew he had won, she knew it.

"Nine hundred," a loud voice spoke up from the back. Kira tried to see through the mass of bodies gathered around, but she couldn't find the bidder, so she watched the auctioneer instead.

Grater must have known him, because his eyes furrowed and he looked surprised at the bid. But he acknowledged it and turned back to Ssirone for the counter-bid.

Kira felt her own smug mile work at her mouth when she noticed Ssirone's disappointment at not being able to see the bidder and intimidate or paralyze him like he had Peter.

"Nine hundred fifty," Ssirone called to Grater, but Kira could hear the panic in his voice. He was about out of money and desperate.

She craned her own head and tried to search the crowd. Who was the new bidder? Was he worse than Peter or Ssirone? Would she get someone like her stepfather? She shuddered and felt the chain around her neck. Had it just gotten tighter? Breathing was suddenly difficult, and her bravado started to wane.

"One thousand freedom tokens," the confident voice answered.

"That'sss too many freedom tokensss to pay for food. I'm out."

Kira silently prayed and hoped for some miraculous intervention. A hole opening up in the middle of the earth to swallow her was her best bet.

She felt the verbal hammer of the word *Sold* as it came crashing down on her. Her head felt so heavy. Despair clung to her thoughts, trying to take control of her soul. The mental battle slammed at her, but she couldn't let go. She wasn't about to let it gain any ground. This moment or circumstance was out of her control, but that didn't mean she was giving up yet.

The giant handed her leash to her new owner, a plump man with thinning dark hair. He yanked on it, forcing her to follow behind him. All she could see was the back of his head and an extravagant robe. She imagined that her eyes were laser beams, boring holes into it.

Her owner handed her to a large redheaded troll while he paid Grater the money due.

Two other people joined them near the gate, and Kira thought she recognized the one in the long jacket. In fact, she knew she did.

"Hey!" Kira called. "Hey!"

He turned suddenly, bringing his face mere inches from hers. "Slaves don't talk unless spoken to." He glanced away quickly as if fearing being associated with her.

"I know you," she said. Butt-Chin's sandy blond hair was long and untrimmed. Nothing about him looked out of place.

He ignored her. That was fine with Kira. She'd never gotten his name and preferred her nickname for him anyway. "Butt-Chin" definitely made him less scary.

He nodded at the boy zeke, standing alone. A look of silent understanding passed between them, and Butt Chin joined the line, waiting to pay and leave. Why didn't the zeke run away? Why wasn't he chained like her?

Her fat owner said, "Come. Now." The troll yanked on her leash. She tried to hold her head high as she left the Gambler's Market, to not show the fear rolling off of her in waves. They escorted Kira back to the docks and boarded another boat. The skiff she'd come in on had been falling to pieces, but the *Siren* was the limo of small boats. Newer, with seats instead of benches, it had a motor.

"Sit." The fat man commanded. "We are waiting for my trainer."

She was going to ask him who that was, when he smiled and she felt the weight of someone getting in the boat. She turned.

Butt-Chin and the zeke.

The owner spread his arms out across the leather seats. "Ah, Den, did you find me a boggart at the market?"

"No, Remus, none with debts came into the market." Den came over and pushed her onto a bench. He tied her to the railing.

So this was Remus? Kira wrinkled her nose with distaste upon learning her new owner's name. Alpo and Vic had mentioned him—with fear. But the slightly overweight man seemed more intent on his next meal and extravagant clothes than on what went on in the slave market.

"Pity, I was really hoping for one." His voice had a whiny sigh to it, but then his eyes roamed over and he caught sight of the zeke.

"Oh, Den. Please don't tell me you spent my money on another zeke. You shouldn't have. I've already got Creeper." His voice hitched as if he was expecting to be presented with a gift. He said it slyly but it was obvious he wanted the zeke.

"No, I bought him with my tokens," Den said stiffly. For a split second, Remus scowled, but then the look disappeared. "I put a bid in for one of Howl's boggarts for you like you asked if I couldn't find you one. We should know within the hour if you've won…but I can already tell you that you probably did."

"Oh goody." Remus chuckled and pressed his fingers together. Large rings glittered on each of his fingers. "I can't wait." Remus surveyed Den's purchase and let out a disappointed sigh. "He looks familiar. Why does he look familiar?"

Den shrugged. "I don't know," he answered dismissively. "I wasn't able to gain much on his background."

"He looks far too young and untried. How can you ever become a revered sponsor like me if you keep buying unknown zekes?" Remus said snidely. "You can't, that's how. As a trainer, you know what you need. You've got to spend your tokens wisely."

Kira watched Den's cheek twitch, his jaw clenched. The zeke's eyes glittered dangerously, but neither spoke up.

"Den, take us home," Remus commanded. He resettled himself on the bench near Kira. He stroked her dirty blond hair gingerly and then gripped her chin hard. "Creeper has a thing for blonds. He says the flavor is like sweet cream. You are his reward for winning the last game."

She pulled her chin out of his grip.

His dull brown eyes narrowed in displeasure, his mouth pressed tight.

Den steered the boat under a bridge and down a dark corridor. There seemed to be less sewage and dead things floating in the water the farther they got from the city. White logs floated in the water, and Kira jumped when they twitched and slid underwater. They weren't logs. They were albino crocodiles. The zeke boy sat on the side and continued to stare at Kira, but he didn't seem as infatuated with her. He seemed more curious.

At least he wasn't looking at her like a Big Mac.

They rode the boat downriver for five minutes before drifting to a stop in front of an iron gate. Den waved a flag and the large gate on creaky hinges slowly rose out of the water. He steered them right through the gate. Kira turned to see only one person operating the lift, but the key was attached to his belt. The sound of the gate lowering into the water made Kira's heart pound faster. There wouldn't be much time left.

She was right. They pulled up to a long dock, and onlookers came out of a large cement compound. Most looked like ordinary slaves, but she immediately spotted the fighters. They were well fed and muscled, with an air of determination and pride.

One stood a foot taller than the rest and had sunken eyes—must be Remus's Creeper. He scanned the boat, his eyes ignoring Den. He studied the boy for a moment with a question in his eyes.

And then he spotted Kira, and a wild almost dangerous aura overtook him.

"Mine!" He growled and knocked his comrades back a few feet. The young zeke in the boat suddenly stood up in challenge, as if willing to battle to the death over fresh meat. Remus's fighter grinned cruelly, but didn't speak again.

Remus stood and pushed the new boy zeke down. He motioned to Den just as he was bringing Kira out of the boat. "I think I'll save you from making a huge career mistake and buy your zeke."

"No, I'd rather not sell." Den spoke calmly, but Kira heard steel in his voice.

"If you want to continue to train for me, you'll do what I say."

Den picked up Kira's chain and led her out of the boat. He just said nonchalantly, "Then I'll have to find another gym."

Remus blinked, clearly displeased that Den was so unfazed by the threat. Finally, he waved his hand at Den. "No, stay…for now. Creeper is the best zeke there is anyway."

He turned to his salivating slave. "Yes, Creeper, this one is for you. Your gift for winning the last event. Now remember, there will be more where this one comes from if you keep winning. Can you do that?"

Creeper looked like he had problems dragging his eyes away from Kira. His body went tense with hunger, and he was salivating everywhere. "Yes, Master, I will keep winning for you." He reached out to grab Kira's arm and pull her towards his room, but she ducked.

Den pretended to trip and dropped her chain. Kira saw her opportunity.

She took it and ran.

***

Creeper smiled as it tore off down the tunnel. It had no idea that it ran toward the training grounds. His personal playground. Catching it would be easy—he was born for it.

Run, girl. Run.

He licked his lips. He imagined the smell of its fear and knew its adrenaline would taste, oh so sweet. With a cry of glee, he launched into an easy pace after his golden-haired prey.

His master yelled after him, "Creeper, stop playing with your food and eat it already!" Creeper laughed hysterically.

FIVE

Maniacal laughter followed Kira down the tunnel, the sound of it chilling her to the bones. She had no choice but to run faster—push herself to her limit. She hadn't eaten in days and was tiring quickly. The bread they'd given her at the Gambler's Market barely touched the gnawing hunger that constantly plagued her.

And there was one other problem. Kira didn't know where she was going. She passed plenty of places to hide, but Kira wasn't interested in hiding. Escape wasn't possible at the moment, and this thing had been told to eat her. She had to kill whatever was chasing her.

Creeper, like the boy zeke, didn't look like your run-of-the-mill bloody, dumb, stagger-walking zombie from Hollywood. The ones always obsessed with eating brains. The two zombies she had now seen were the opposite; they looked completely human, definitely weren't dumb, and their speed was incredible.

Her muscles burned, but she ignored the pain to veer left down a corridor that opened into an old indoor vehicle graveyard. The cars and trucks spread across the large space like they were set up to be used as part of an obstacle course. Her first instinct told her to keep running, but there was opportunity here. She ran in a zig zag pattern and ducked between an old tour bus and a classic Mustang. Lying on the ground, she searched under the chassis for approaching feet.

Creeper laughed when he ran into the room. "There's nowhere to run, my sweet, except into my arms."

What a terrifying endearment. Kira strained to listen for movement but couldn't hear anything over her own panicked breathing. With shaking hands, she covered her mouth to silence the sound. She almost missed it, the hollow sound of popping metal. He was crawling onto a car. From a high enough view point he'd be able to see her.

There it was again. Another popping sound.

Closer.

Kira gathered the chain to her body, pushed off with her hands, and rolled quickly underneath the bus, trying to plan her next move. The popping sounds were getting faster and louder. Rhythmic. Creeper had to be running across the hoods of the cars in a direct course towards her. Had he heard the chain rattle?

She spotted an emergency access panel, but she would need time and a distraction. She looked around for a weapon—and found a large rock. That wouldn't help her. Or could it?

Rolling to the other side of the bus, Kira crouched by the tire and threw the rock as far as she could in the opposite direction. It wasn't a good throw, and it thudded softly against the side of a Chevy. Holding her breath, she waited as the sounds of pursuit stopped. She could see Creeper standing on top of a blue Volkswagen beetle, his head cocked in confusion as he stared where the rock had hit.

She froze and held her breath; she was too scared to move. Mentally, she urged him on. *Follow the rock. I'm over there.* He must have gotten her mental message, because he turned and flew in the direction of the sound. Kira didn't have much time. She'd only lobbed the rock a hundred feet. Silently, she scrambled under the bus and pulled the knob, twisting it to release the access panel.

It wouldn't budge. Biting her lip, she kneeled and tried to push it open. Something was blocking it from inside.

This couldn't be happening.

It moved.

Foregoing all efforts at being quiet, she shoved, grunting as the door inched forward. Kira peeked into the empty tour bus and saw the broken bench seat that had fallen over and obstructed the panel. As quietly as possible, she slipped inside, closed the panel, and moved the seat back over the door.

The bus was huge—the type with a bathroom and TVs made for traveling cross-country—except without the TV and most of the seats. Kira didn't delude herself into thinking she could hide here forever. She'd made quite a commotion getting in the bus. Creeper would probably be here any second.

Keeping low to the floor, she moved to the front of the bus and searched for keys. In the ignition, the cup holder—nothing. She only had one option—something she'd learned on the street. Kira pulled off the panel under the steering column and eyed the three wires running into the cylinder. Quickly, she disconnected them and grabbed a piece of metal from one of the broken seats. She began to strip the protective covering over the wires. Sweat poured down her forehead, and her fingers fumbled with the exposed wires.

Now she just had to guess which wires she needed. She touched the black wire to the red one, and the bus lights flicked on. The radio blared country music, and she switched off the radio. Her cover was blown.

A quick peek over the dashboard showed her Creeper on the hood of a car fifty feet in front of her. He grinned in triumph and jumped off.

And charged toward the bus.

Kira ducked and grabbed the other two wires and flicked them together. Pain raced up her arms as they sparked, and she heard the engine rumble to life—then die. Blood pooled in her mouth. Must've bitten her lip with the shock. Her hands trembled as she flicked them together again and held them when the bus roared to life. Biting back the pain, she twisted the black wire and the red starter wire together and slid into the driver's seat.

"Come on, you piece of garbage!" Kira shouted as she shifted the bus into first gear and floored it. The bus roared and barreled forward, taking off the rear bumper of a Buick. Creeper stalled in his tracks when he noticed the bus racing towards him. There was nowhere to go; he was trapped between two towering stacks of metal cars.

Kira screamed and closed her eyes as she hit the zombie full force. She didn't want to look, not even when she continued to push the pedal to the floor, trying to slam him into the cars and walls in front of her. Only one of them would come out of this alive, and that was going to be her, because he had to be already dead.

The bus plowed through two more cars before crashing into the wall, pinning Creeper between the grill and two tons of cement. The impact threw Kira forward into the steering wheel. Shards of glass, metal, and chunks of plastic rained down on her, and blood streamed from her forehead into her eyes, obscuring her vision. Pain radiated from her stomach and legs.

Where is it?

She had hit Creeper and then driven the bus straight into the wall. She tried to look up, but…there was smoke? Why was there smoke?

Spots swam in front of her, an acrid electrical smell burning her nostrils. She tried to move but was pinned between the steering wheel and seat. Kira coughed and covered her mouth with her dirty t-shirt as more noxious smoke began to choke her.

She twisted again and cried out in pain when a three inch glass shard imbedded itself deeper into her side. She had to get out before she burned alive or, more likely, died from smoke inhalation. Kira reached forward and found the lever to adjust the steering wheel. It moved an inch, just enough for her to slide to the floor. She pulled on the door lever, and it swung partway open.

She squeezed through. Grabbing the wound in her side, Kira turned and ran—but not before she confirmed Creeper was dead. His legs stuck out from under the bus. Definitely not moving.

Kira plodded slowly towards a dark hole in the wall, hoping it was a tunnel that led to freedom or escape. An explosion rocked the cavern as the bus erupted in flames. The force from the blast knocked Kira face first into the dirt and she lay there stunned and disoriented, ears ringing.

When the ringing stopped, she heard voices from down the tunnel. They would be on their way to investigate the explosion.

She couldn't be in the open.

She dragged her body through the mud into a crevice between two beat up cars. As she glanced back over her shoulder, she spotted a blood trail in the dirt—that led directly to her hiding spot. It was too late to do anything now.

"Find the human and bring it to me! She will pay for killing my prized zeke." Remus strung curses together like Christmas lights. "How could that little pipsqueak of a human do this much damage? She actually ruined my training course. Creeper would never"—more swearing—"Explosions weren't Creeper's style."

Kira stayed low, as still as she could.

***

Remus checked the wreckage twice to make sure it really was Creeper pinned between the wall and bus and that he was totally, completely dead. There was no paying to bring him back now.

"You, you, and you, put out that fire before it reaches another gas tank." Blast that girl. If it hadn't killed Creeper, he could have paid Warrick to bring him back from half-dead. Not even Warrick could bring them back from all-dead.

Remus spun and kicked the hellhound that sat by his side, as if he hadn't already gotten his instructions. "I told you, you blasted dog. Find that human." The dog yelped and snarled back, nipping the air in anger. The demon dog took off running, sniffing the air for the human girl.

It was probably useless, though. The toxic fumes in the air would cover her scent. The hellhound paused, look back at Remus, then took off slowly down the tunnel towards home. He must've decided to sniff in a fresher environment, one that didn't burn his nose.

Well, even if he had to take care of it himself, Remus would make sure that girl died. He'd just do it later. After his peons put out the fire and cleared the air.

***

Something large passed Kira, only five feet from where she was hiding. It turned around and came back.

Pain seared her side so deeply, she almost cried out for help, not even caring if it was another man-eating monster that found her. At least if it was, it would kill her and end her pain.

The large beast tracking her blood trail stopped in front of her hiding hole.

Kira could only see the feet, but she had to blink her eyes in confusion when she saw four hooves. Loud crunching noises came from above her as the car sheltering her was hefted and pushed to the side. It spun on its roof slowly like a top.

Kira shielded her face from the beast with her hands to avoid the oncoming death blow.

But warm hands grabbed her instead, pulling her up. Something lifted her off of the ground and held her against its bare chest.

Panicked, Kira pushed away. Its strangely human face startled her. The man-thing carried her away from the noise and panic of the fire. Some monsters continued to search for her, while others tried to put out the flames.

She didn't see Remus.

Was this guy handing her over to him?

He ducked through an exit she hadn't seen.

And the pattern of the creature's movement was wrong—odd. Kira peered more closely at the man's face, glanced at his human chest and then behind him for the answer. The thing that was carrying her had a man's upper torso and a horse's body.

"You have hooves! Are you a horse or man?" Kira didn't mean to let the words slip out, but with the nauseating pain in her stomach and the ringing in her ears he could hardly fault her.

"I'm both," the rich velvety voice answered back. "I am a centaur."

She sputtered out one last thought. "Giddyup."

SIX

The centaur—Warrick, he said his name was—was killing her. Not literally, but if Kira had to drink another nasty concoction, she knew she was going to die. He pushed another cup of green tonic towards her, the fifth in the last hour.

"You need to drink this every ten minutes. I told you it will help with the smoke inhalation." Warrick stared at Kira hard until she gave in and swallowed the contents of the cup in one gulp. She made an ugly face at him in return. A few seconds later, Kira was coughing again and spitting up black and gray phlegm. Her body ached, and she wouldn't be surprised if her sutured wound was bleeding again.

"It's nasty," she said between wracks of coughing.

"Yes, but it is helping." He smirked before taking the cup from her and putting it on the table.

Warrick had carried Kira to a small building a quarter-mile away. He lived in a simple house with no roof. But then who needed a roof when it never rained or snowed underground? The layout was very open and included an area covered in straw, table, and chairs. She had spent plenty of time on that examining table when

Warrick brought her in a few hours ago. He took care of the wound in her side right away, then bandaged the cut above her eye, and now was treating her for smoke inhalation.

"You know you didn't have to do this, right?" Kira looked away from the large centaur guiltily. She was finding it really hard not to stare at him, like she would stare at a unicorn. He was beautiful. His coat was a warm brown that matched his skin. His ears pointed and stuck out from his long braided black hair.

"It's what I do. I am a healer. I abhor all death and violence unless it comes at the cost of protecting the herd." He went to the cupboard and started to prepare food. Kira had to drag her eyes away from the loaf of bread he was slicing. "Not all of us in this land are monsters."

"You could have fooled me," Kira replied in a snarky tone. "Your people kidnapped me, sold me to a slave trader, and then tried to feed me to a zombie."

"Zeke," Warrick corrected. "And you see how well that turned out, don't you? You aren't the one that is dead."

"Zombies are already dead," Kira snapped back.

Warrick brought a plate with sliced bread and cheese and set it before Kira. She waited until he motioned with his head for her to eat. Then, she snatched three pieces of bread and cheese from the plate before realizing she'd taken almost all of it. She could have given some of it back, but then thought better. She was the one that was injured and starved; she needed it more than he did.

Warrick watched her shove the bread into her mouth. He sighed sadly. "He was only half-dead. Zekes are the cursed ones, or half-dead. And don't call them zombies. That's going to get you in a lot of trouble if you plan to survive long. And it wasn't my people. I don't know if you noticed, but there are a lot of gods and races coexisting down here, scraping a living, trying to survive. You can't bunch us all into the same group."

Kira felt duly chastised. It was the same in her world. People assumed all homeless people were low-life drunks or drug addicts. "I'm sorry."

"Apology accepted." Warrick went to his table and began to clean his instruments. He didn't wash them in the sink or sterilize them, but pulled out a metal flask and dropped a few droplets of silver liquid on the tweezers, needles, and table. The bits of blood disappeared instantaneously, and a strong mint smell wafted through the room.

"What is that?" Kira asked.

"Never you mind." Warrick quickly pocketed the flask in a pouch he wore on his leather belt. Kira knew from earlier that there were many flasks inside—he'd used a different one on her wound. He told her it was unicorn tears, but she was surprised when he clammed up about the flask he'd just used. Was it illegal? Expensive?

That was something worth keeping in mind for later.

Kira finished her bread and cheese and grabbed the last two pieces from the plate as she stood up to leave. "Well, thank you for your hospitality and fixing me up and stuff, but I think it's time for me to go. So if you would be so kind as to point me toward the surface, I'll be going.

"Can't." Warrick walked in front of her and blocked the door.

"Can't point me to the surface or can't let me go?" Kira stood with her hands at her sides. She stepped back, away from the centaur and felt around for a weapon.

"Both. What did you think would happen? That I would patch you up and help you escape? No, I can't do that. I told you that we are all here trying to survive, and Remus owns me." He pointed to the band on his wrist. "You, whether you agree to it or not, are his property and must be returned to him."

She flung her hands in the air and yelled at Warrick. "Then why not turn me over right when you found me? Why go to all of the trouble to feed me and heal me!" She circled around and came to the table.

"Because if I would have turned you in at that moment, Remus could have killed you instantly, without even thinking. I hoped that delaying your capture, I'd buy you some time. You took the life of one of his fighters outside of a game. He has every right to demand your life in exchange."

"He was trying to take my life outside of a game! Kill or be killed! Or maybe those same rules don't apply to me?"

"They don't. You're human. You don't have rights down here. Our laws don't work in your favor. But I don't think it's your fate to die here today."

"You lie!" Kira grabbed the glass from the table and threw it hard at Warrick's head. He ducked, and it smashed against the door. "You are not a healer; you are some sort of sick, demented torturer! You planned this from the beginning." Kira moved over by the couch, beside a window.

Movement outside alerted her to visitors. Her heart dropped. Two very large doglike creatures with red eyes were sniffing a path right to the door. Den, Remus, and a large ogre were on the dogs' trail.

Warrick saw them at the same time. "They're here. They were faster than I thought." He shifted uncomfortably and wouldn't look at Kira.

"You were wrong," she seethed between clenched teeth. "You are worse than the monsters."

Warrick must have changed his mind, because he suddenly moved into action and went to a trunk. A long howl pierced the darkness as the dogs began to circle the house and growl at the door. Warrick tossed clothes, books, and various items on the floor until he pulled out a small-sheathed knife. "Quick, hide this. Don't use it now; don't ever let them know you have it." He tossed it toward her.

With a deft, one-handed catch, she plucked it out of the air and hid it in her boot.

She stayed down a moment to re-lace her boot, and Warrick rushed her, clamping a wet cloth over her mouth. Struggling proved worthless. The smell was too much and…she went limp in his arms. Her world went black.

SEVEN

Warrick hefted her feather-light body and once again pondered how she'd ended up down here. He slid her, unconscious, onto his examining table seconds before the pounding on the door.

"Open up, Warrick. I know it's in there." Remus yelled at the closed wooden door.

Warrick paused in front of the door as if debating. He pulled open the door but stood in the frame, blocking Remus access. The man never hid his intentions. Warrick knew his soul was damned, but he had to respect him as owner.

"Warrick, you fool, move." Remus pushed hard against the centaur's chest, but he didn't budge.

"It's over there," he spoke quietly. "It's still alive."

Remus narrowed his eyes at Warrick, watching him. "Let me see it, and I'll be the judge."

Warrick moved aside as Remus stepped into the room, followed by Den. With the two intimidating men there, it seemed like the room shrank in size. Remus marched over to Kira's prone form lying on the table. He leaned forward, mere inches from her body and studied her closely. "How long has she been unconscious?"

"Since I found her," Warrick lied easily. There was nothing in his code of morals that said lying was wrong, especially when lying to someone cruel enough to be Satan's brother.

But he was careful to not glance at Den. The trainer had recently lost everything because of his gambling, and he was on the cusp of either salvation or damnation. Warrick had heard he was trying to put his life back together. But there was little he could do to help Den at this point. He couldn't let that man's soul be on his conscious anymore.

That's why he had tried to save the human girl at the last minute. He needed to worry about her soul.

Remus picked at a morsel of bread on Kira's shirt and held it up in the air. "Did you get hungry, Warrick? It's not like you to eat while treating a patient."

Warrick was proud that he didn't shift his weight or look away as he lied again. "It's not a patient, but a thing. It doesn't warrant the same respect as us."

Remus stared around the room and then back at Kira's body. Without warning, he opened his fist and smacked the girl hard across the face, clearly surprised when she didn't jump up or scream. He even leaned down to sniff her mouth.

***

Den had stood back, observing. He could tell by the centaur's tense muscles, he was lying. But it didn't matter. Den didn't want Remus to kill the girl either. He probably would have lied as well, in Warrick's shoes.

But to what end was Warrick working? Why would he risk Remus's wrath?

Warrick's medical kit was out, and an old trunk was left open. He spied the centaur's holy candle and prayer book half-hidden in the trunk and rolled his eyes. Of course, he'd try and save her, because he felt responsible for the death of his herd. Their souls weighed on him, he said. Den frowned as he looked over at Warrick. If only the centaur understood. Some people just couldn't be saved.

"Can you wake her? I want her to be awake when I kill her for destroying Creeper." Remus quivered with a weird mix of anticipation and anger.

"I can, but she won't be coherent. The drugs I used on her will still be in her system; she won't know what is happening." The centaur pulled out a vial and lifted Kira's head as if to pour it down her throat. He glanced over at Den and must've known he saw right through Warrick.

"That doesn't do me any good. I want the wretched slave to suffer. I have no hope of winning the next event without Creeper, and Plutus won't wait long before he calls in my debt. I need more freedom tokens." Remus paced the small house with his hands behind his back. "You worthless piece of cow, get out of my sight. You're lucky I don't feed you to the hungry runners."

Den shifted against the wall, watching. He suspected Remus was capable of a lot more than he liked others to believe. So Den needed to keep his wits, reveal nothing.

Warrick gathered his things and exited the front door. Remus pounded his fist on the table. "You owe me, Den. You owe me for what your new slave did to my property. I demand retribution."

"You're right, Remus. But I'll buy you another zeke." Den nodded, as if convincing himself he owed that to Remus. "A better one, a stronger one. You don't want mine. You said yourself, he looks young."

Remus looked up thoughtfully. "That may be good, but it's not enough. The human thing can't go unpunished. I think I'll feed it to the trolls."

"No," Den whispered. A glow flickered from his band. Already? Thankfully, it drew Remus's attention away from the slip. Why had he even said that? He glanced down.

Each of them held up his arm and watched his bracer impatiently.

Remus breathed deeply through his nose. "It can't be me. I don't owe that much."

Den saw it wasn't a debtor's mark being broadcasted across their bands. "It's a lottery, but why already?"

The flashing quickened, and he knew that every registered being in Underland was currently staring at their band. Waiting to see who would be selected for the next game.

The Underlords were forcing more and more of these random drafts—anyone was possible. What were the Underlords after exactly? The games were effective enough on their own. They'd been crowning many champions.

The white blinking slowed on Den's band and went out.

Remus gave a delighted cry. "I knew it wouldn't be me."

But there was another light in the room that hadn't dimmed. Den looked over at the young human girl and sighed. Her band hadn't gone out. He'd never seen someone chosen so fast. She had only been in the registry for a short time, and now he was going to lose her. She'd been nothing more than bad luck ever since he met her. "She's a blight on everything she touches."

"Ha! It must be my lucky day." He rubbed his hands together. "The gods have decided its fate for me." Remus smiled cruelly. "When did you say I'll get my boggart from Howl?"

More than likely, the human girl would die competing. Still, giving her a fighting chance was better than giving her none. Den rubbed the back of his neck. "It's been confirmed you won the bid. Howl will bring him to you next week."

"Ah, which one? Who did I get?"

"Bogeyman."

"Oh, Bogeyman is vicious—and he didn't compete in the last game, if I remember correctly. Yes! He will tear the little human apart." Remus slapped the table in triumph before leaning down to whisper into Kira's unhearing ears in a sing song voice. "Run little human, run as fast as you can. You can't outrun my new Bogeyman."

EIGHT

Kira knew she was in trouble the moment the door opened and Den walked into her one room cell. Hours earlier, she'd awakened in the stark, sterile room and panicked. Every muscle in her body had screamed to fight, but there were no enemies present. She was alone except for the two metal frame beds and a nightstand—both bolted to the ground.

She'd pounded on the huge metal door, paced, and sat in the corner staring at the exit, willing it to open so she could escape. Sheer luck had kept her alive up to this point. She was surprised Warrick hadn't killed her in her sleep. Why had he betrayed her at the last minute? Whatever it took, she'd get her revenge on the four-footed doctor.

She sat on one of the beds and scooted back into the corner. Plotting, planning, waiting. That had been her morning. Not to mention that annoying white light on her band that had been blinking non-stop for the last hours. It was probably malfunctioning. She'd been trying to figure out how to get it off when Den surprised her by opening the door.

He was wearing the long black jacket that reached almost to the stone floor, the same one she had seen him wear in the boat. His blond hair was tousled from running his hand through it. Thick calf-high boots completed the somber ensemble. He frowned at her back-to-the-wall position.

Kira glowered at him, refusing to move or show fear of any kind. He approached and stopped three feet from her huddled form.

Turning around, he gestured to the room. "Do you like? It's better than the cage." His hands reached towards the front of his jacket, and he began to unbutton a few of the straps.

Kira stiffened, wishing she had never trapped herself in the corner of the room. How stupid could she be?

Den held his hands in the air. "Hey now, don't be scared." He reached back toward the strap and slowly undid the buckle across the front. His hand disappeared inside a pocket. He pulled out a metal stamp and reached for her wrist.

She yanked her arm away and leaned harder against the wall, pulling her feet up toward her.

"Scared of a stamp? I wouldn't expect such a childish reaction from someone who killed one of the top fighters." He grabbed her arm, and set the stamp on her bracer. When he pressed a small button on the top, the stamp turned red hot, like a car lighter. Smoke rolled up into the air as it burned a design into the metal.

He pulled back. As the smoke cleared, Kira saw an emblem burned into her bracer. "What is it?"

"It's your brand—Remus's brand, to be exact." He pointed toward the eagle holding two arrows in its claws. It looked very much like the eagle on the American dollar, except that this eagle looked way tougher and it was missing something—the branch in its left claw.

"What, no olive branch?" Why had he chosen such a patriotic emblem?

Den shook his head. "Down here, peace doesn't get you very far. The people only understand one thing: fighting. Using the olive branch would have been taken as a symbol of weakness. He can't have that."

"No, we can't be pansies and show compassion or mercy with a bunch of monsters."

Den locked eyes with her. "No. No, we can't, because deep down—no matter our exteriors—we are all monsters."

He was being civil, and she'd just opened her mouth and insulted him. "I'm sorry, I didn't mean you." Her voice filled with regret. "Thank you. For helping me."

He stiffened as if he was offended by her gratitude. "I shouldn't have."

"Then why did you? Why did you drop my chain when Remus sent Creeper after me?"

"You deserved a fighting chance. But you—I—you're just getting in the way of my plans."

He flipped her wrist over so she could see the digital screen and the runes. "If you try and run away, he can track you with it. There's only two ways it releases from your wrist: Get Remus to release ownership of you. Or get freedom tokens. Red means you own nothing—or you're in debt. Earn enough, and you'll be free." He moved over to the door and unlocked it.

"How do I get Remus to release me?" Kira could feel the blood rushing to her ears with apprehension.

"You don't. Remus has never given up any of his slaves. Ever. Just the great kind of guy Remus is." Den stepped toward the door. "Listen, I'm going to let you out of the cell, let you explore a little, since you don't have long anyway. My advice? Stay low, don't make a scene. Just try and stay alive. One day at a time."

Her mind was spinning. "Let's say, hypothetically, I could get him to release me. How do I earn freedom tokens?"

He rolled his eyes. "Like everyone else down here." He looked at the white blinking light. "The ga—" He bit his lip. "Menial labor." He'd definitely been about to say something else. "But don't waste your time trying to escape. Save yourself the energy. You're registered. Marked."

"I don't understand."

"You belong to our world now. Underland. This is where you'll die. Even if by some miracle you live, no one will ever allow you back to the surface world. No one would risk you exposing our secrets."

With that, he left.

Kira sat forward, stunned. She really was trapped here. Granted, she now had more freedom to move about outside of the small cell, but it wasn't much more than an illusion.

She couldn't waste any more time in her room.

She looked at the doorway and the darkness beyond and debated what lay before her. She'd seen many slaves roaming freely when they pulled up in the boat to the compound; each of them had an arm brace as well. Soft padding footsteps alerted her to movement outside her door. Kira stiffened and cursed herself for not running out that door when she had the chance. She was now once again trapped in the cell. Her side wasn't hurting badly at all, so that would help. What had the centaur used on her wounds anyway?

The footsteps got closer, and a body slowed and stopped in her doorway. It was the boy zeke.

He looked almost as surprised to see her in the room as she was to see him. Kira held her breath, waiting for the hungry zeke to rush in and attack her. She let her hands fall to her sides but kept them clenched and ready.

The boy gave her an impervious look and then kept walking, ignoring her, to continue on his journey down the hall. He looked right through her. She could have been a fly on the wall for all of the attention he just gave her.

Shocked and confused, Kira gingerly crept from the bed, careful to not make any loud creaks on the springs. She moved to the door just as carefully and put her back to it.

Time for a peek down the hall. A single bare bulb hung at the far left end, illuminating a set of metal stairs—stairs the zeke was currently navigating downwards. To the right was an endless array of doors, some opened, some closed—all numbered. Kira didn't know what other monsters might be residing on the other side of those metal doors, and she didn't want to find out. The safest route seemed to be following the zeke, which she did.

At a safe distance.

The young man stopped once and looked up through the grates above him. Kira pressed herself against the wall, in the shadows, and waited. Hoping he hadn't heard her.

"It's all right; I'm not going to eat you. I've got more important things to take care of." His voice had a warm, almost husky, tone, which really could have made girls swoon. If he weren't the cannibal type.

"Good to know, I guess. But what about later…" Kira let the words trail off and walked down the steps after him, still keeping a reasonable distance.

He shrugged and brushed the brown hair out of his eyes. "I guess later will depend on how much you annoy me and how hungry I get." His smile didn't reach his eyes. Kira inwardly cringed, but was careful to keep her emotions equally unreadable.

He waited as she approached, staring at her eye to eye, as if daring her to respond. When she didn't, he frowned slightly.

She'd won the silent challenge.

Feeling braver, she passed him on the steps and walked through a set of double doors leading outside to an enclosed courtyard. Instead of grass, it was covered in moss, probably the only thing that would grow under the fluorescent lights. Over to one side, a large group of monsters lifted weights, wrestling and showing off. Smaller humanoid monsters ran after them carrying trays with drinks, snacks, and towels. Each of the smaller monsters had a length of tattoos and designs starting behind the ear and running down the side of the neck. Their hair had been either shaven or pulled into a braided design—apparently to keep the tattoos visible. These were obviously the slaves, meant to cater to the tougher looking monsters.

Throughout the commons area, benches and couches were positioned for gathering, some facing multiple screens that lined one wall. What channels could they possibly get deep underground? And what kind of segments did monsters like watching? A few tattered rugs were placed awkwardly around the encampment in an attempt to make everything look homier.

It didn't work.

Kira almost let her fear freeze her in her tracks, but she held her head high, like she belonged with the monsters, and walked steadily towards a distant table with food. Every fiber of her being was telling her to get as far from them as possible, to run away, escape. But the hunter side of Kira knew that if she did, if she bolted and ran, it would cause even more notice—possibly ending in another chase and death.

The zeke boy also aimed for the table.

***

The girl tried to look like she didn't care what was going on around her. He almost laughed out loud when she entered the courtyard and froze, face to face with some of the scariest monsters she'd probably ever seen. He watched her square her shoulders and march straight into their midst.

He liked that. He liked her bravado at the slave market, and even their encounter in the stairwell. When Creeper had taken off after her, he really thought that would be the end of her. He'd almost stood and challenged him for her right then. But it would mess up his plan if he got in an altercation too early.

It pained him to let her go, and he was surprised when he met her in the stairwell. Den had said she survived and killed Creeper, but he hadn't expected her to be out wandering around. It made him respect and like her even more.

She intrigued him, and almost nothing intrigued him anymore—but she couldn't distract him. Right now, he had to lay low.

The girl moved in front of him and he caught a whiff of her scent. He closed his eyes and inhaled the tantalizing aroma of her skin. He really had to stop thinking of her. She was making a beeline for the table of food. He didn't know what possessed him to follow her, because he wasn't at all hungry for that kind of food. Still, it had been a while since he'd eaten something warm. *Don't focus on the girl. Ignore her. Don't get involved.*

But then, behind him, he heard the witch start to shout. He turned.

Kira stared at the table of food.

All activity came to a standstill. Heads swerved to look at her, and a few laughed cruelly. Kira swallowed, but kept walking toward the long tables of food. A slave scuttled out of the way as Kira glared angrily in her direction. She was decent at not showing fear. But she had to be afraid. He sat down to watch.

***

Seriously, this girl—whoever she was—better not get in the way with her food. Kira was hungry.

"Is that the one?" a feminine voice asked. Kira glanced sideways. The voice belonged to a young girl with tight black braids wound up on the sides of her head. She wore a black jacket and a short skirt and leggings, and she sat on a pool table next to a large feline man. Others lounged around the table as well, but no one was actually playing.

The girl's furry cheetah-colored companion nodded in answer and glanced towards Kira. He stood on two legs and had human-looking facial features and arms, but that's where the likeness ended. His powerfully built legs were long and lean, and a black-tipped tail swished silently behind him.

"I don't believe you, Chaz." The girl jumped down from the pool table and pointed at Kira. "Tell me you are joking! There is no way in Underland that piece of dog food had the strength and cunning to kill our best fighter."

Kira reached the food and picked out the least spoiled fruit from a bowl. And a heel of bread. There was also a large kettle of soup, and platters of meat—cooked no less—but since she couldn't guarantee the animal was one she knew, it was probably best to go vegetarian.

She glanced over at a nearby bench and spotted the zeke boy, joining the other monsters with his food. A few even slid over to give him room. Kira stayed at the table to eat. The food was stale and the fruit bitter, but she swallowed every bite, keeping an eye on the upset girl and an ear on the mob.

"That *tramp* couldn't have been the one that killed Creeper!" The girl's voice rose with every word, and her hands started to become more animated. A few others joined her group. Whatever they said seemed to make her angrier.

Kira turned away and hoped that by ignoring them, pretending to be oblivious to their complaints, she could avoid a confrontation.

"Hey, you!"

So she was wrong.

Kira kept her back straight and pretended to not hear the girl. When quick hands knocked the food out of her grip, making it fall on the ground, Kira turned, seeing red—and the irritating girl.

Her smile was smug. "Slaves don't eat with the fighters. You eat after we're done."

Kira bit her tongue and picked up another a slice of bread to begin the process of replacing the food she had dropped. This time she was anticipating Mouthy to try and knock her food away again. The girl shot out an arm, and Kira deftly blocked it with her forearm. Then she turned, grabbed the girl's wrist, and shoved her away.

The girl blinked in surprise but quickly regained her bad-girl composure. "Don't you touch me, slave. Don't you know you shouldn't touch your betters?"

Kira raised one eyebrow in disbelief. She let her voice drip with sarcasm. "If I see someone better than me, I'll remember that."

"Why you little piece of trash!" the girl spat out.

Chaz's ears went back against his head and he snarled at Kira, tensing to pounce.

The girl held up her hand to him. "I'll kill her myself!" Fast as lightning, the girl pulled a set of nunchucks from her belt and swung it at Kira's skull.

This time, Kira dropped her own food to defend herself. The nunchucks cracked loudly against her arm, and pain raced up her arm. She couldn't help wincing, but better her arm than her head. She needed to move.

Kira leapt onto the table with food and ran between the serving dishes piled high as she tried to put distance between herself and her attacker. A few monsters grumbled and complained when Kira's boot smashed their dinner, but not enough to make them stop eating.

The girl was right behind her, swinging her chucks like some sort of video game character.

Except that the pattern she swung them in didn't make sense. It looked like she was using the chucks to draw a symbol in the air.

Oh. She was—the symbol glowed bright green. When the girl screamed, a blast of air came hurtling toward Kira and knocked her off her feet. She flew across the room, breaking another table. *Man that hurt.* Whatever that girl did, Kira couldn't let her do it again.

Pushing her body off the split tabletop, her hand brushed the broken table leg. Kira instinctively gripped it. Just as another attack came—a blast of fire rushed at her—she rolled. A second later, it hit the exact spot she'd landed. The metal popped and sizzled from the intense heat.

Kira knew she couldn't outrun the witch, so she changed directions and charged the girl, holding the table leg out in front of her like a spear.

The witch fumbled for a moment, surprised by the sudden change of tactic. Kira tested the weight of the table leg again—pretty well balanced—and decided to use it like a fighting stick. She swung at the girl's head. The witch blocked it with her nunchucks. Kira rotated the staff and feinted toward her mid-section. She spun it high and feinted toward the head.

The witch kept backing up, trying to block her attack. All Kira wanted was to keep the onslaught steady so the witch couldn't form another spell with her weapon.

***

Impossible. Remus stared out the window across the compound at the fight below. This smug human kept fighting, acting as if it had a right to live.

A gurgle drew Remus's attention back to the screens in the hive. Here, on the bank of monitors, were the vitals of each of his runners. He watched the little blips of their heartbeats and rubbed his hand across the closest black screen. How little they knew, how little they controlled. They were like busy little bees, and he reaped all of their hard work. It was good to be king.

But he knew that there were those that conspired against him. Wanted what was rightfully his. He didn't like it when people stole. He hated thieves, and more than that, he hated liars.

The gurgling came from the floor again. He wished the man would just shut up and die. Remus had almost lost this one. He'd been hiding his winnings and was about to earn his freedom.

No one left without his permission. No one. Earning freedom without his permission equaled an escape attempt. And he could freely punish any of his runners that try and escape.

A knock at the door interrupted his thoughts.

Den.

Den paused and stared at the man moaning on the floor, foam bubbling at his mouth. Remus watched for Den's reaction. Den met Remus's eyes and—there. He saw it. A flicker of disgust followed by hatred. That wouldn't do. Den certainly tried to hide it quickly, but the fact that it had been there at all bothered him. He really hated it when his trainer acted better than everyone. He'd been a little too smug lately, too independent. He had forgotten his roots, where he came from.

"You called me?" Den asked, his face becoming blank.

"One moment, Den." Remus turned to stare at the screen again and watched as the heartbeat he was monitoring sped up. The blips got faster and faster until they flat lined. Remus smiled when the struggling sounds stopped. He reached down to remove the bracer from the dead runner's arm. It was still warm, but he didn't care.

"This one tried to run away, so I terminated his career," Remus explained.

Den's eyes darkened but he didn't respond, which meant dissension. Lack of respect for his way.

"We need to discuss your future here, Den." Remus walked back to the window and looked out across the compound. He waited for Den to come and stand beside him. Remus knew the instant he spotted the human causing a ruckus down below because his posture stiffened.

"How can I trust you to train my runners if you can't even control one human? If it messes up any more of my people, or dies before the challenge"—Remus held up the now vacant brace—"I'll find a way to send you to the ring."

Den rushed out the door, leaping over the dead body. Remus turned and watched as the human attacked his witch. This wouldn't do at all.

He couldn't wait to get rid of them—both.

***

After a few minutes, Kira figured out the witch girl was mostly show. She couldn't hold her ground in a real physical altercation. Kira feinted for the head and then swung the table leg around to sweep her legs out from under her. The girl squealed and lost hold of the nunchucks.

Kira's boot came down hard on her hand as she reached for the weapon. She jabbed the broken end of the pole within inches of the girl's exposed throat. "Threaten me again and I *will* kill you!" Kira snarled out, baring her teeth in anger.

Kira felt different this time. She'd never gotten worried about this encounter. She actually liked the adrenaline rush, the whole sordid fight.

"I…w-we, n-need to get revenge for Creeper." The girl's vibrant green eyes were wet with unshed tears.

"What's your name?" Kira asked.

"Holly." She lay still, unmoving, the smart thing to do.

"Well, Holly, that confrontation will happen on a different day, with a level playing field. No, behind-the-back sneak attacks. Got it?" Kira couldn't blame the girl for wanting revenge, and it wasn't her place to deny it, but she could lay down some boundaries.

The girl's head bobbed in affirmation.

Kira wasn't stupid, she noticed the way Holly's eyes kept flickering between her nunchucks and Chaz standing behind her.

Chaz gave Kira a nod of respect and backed away.

Kira took her boot off Holly's neck and purposely turned her back on the girl. She kept a firm grip on the table leg. With an eye on the shadows and an ear toward the onlookers, she knew the instant Holly acted stupid. Kira swung the table leg in an arc, knocking the weapon from Holly's hand as it was poised to come down on Kira's head. She grabbed a surprised Holly by the front of her jacket and dropped the table leg to the ground.

"I warned you." Kira pulled back her arm to inflict punishment.

Holly looked up into Kira's eyes, weirdly mesmerized. Well, Kira would give her something to look at then.

Her fist.

Kira had only a moment to enjoy her victory before she was thrown to the ground by a mob. Deafening roars, a freakish combination of cat's screech, bull mooing, and high pitched screams filled her ears. Claws scratched at her, hooves kicked her in the sides as Kira tried to roll away from the attackers, but she knew what was coming and mentally prepared herself for the pain.

She dove into the past.

When she had turned twelve, a man wearing a uniform came to their door with a letter, bearing the news that her dad would not be coming back from his latest assignment. For the first time in years, Kira cried. She gave the letter to her mom, and watched as Ellie turned pale and collapsed. Something inside her mother had finally snapped.

It took weeks for Ellie to leave the house after the funeral; she was an emotional wreck, crying and roaming the house as if searching for something or someone. The doctors gave her tons of medications which helped nothing.

Ellie left one night and didn't come home for ten days. Kira had survived just fine without her. But when she finally returned, a man was with her mom.

"This is Bernie, your new father... er stepfather," Ellie announced, clearly drunk.

Her mother had done the unthinkable; she drove to Vegas, got wasted, and married the first jerk to propose to her, for better or for worse.

It was worse.

Bernie was large, fat, and reeked of stale beer. Kira never saw him work and assumed he and Ellie lived off her dad's life insurance policy. Bernie was also a drunk, and lucky Kira, the little fighter, got to be the recipient of his quick temper. When she was thirteen, he pushed her down the stairs for talking back to him; she got eight stitches in her forehead. When she was fourteen, he broke her arm for not taking out the trash. Then came the beatings for talking back. Her mother couldn't protect her. No one could.

Kira was back in that house all over again.

Reliving every punch, kick and broken bone.

One of the beasts launched through the air to land on Kira's back and pin her to the ground. She tried desperately to buck it off, but it had a steel grip around her waist. She tried curling up in a ball.

More punches came, but they didn't land anywhere where she could feel them. Actually, she could feel someone breathing down her neck. And she heard quiet grunts of pain, coming from above her.

The monster wrapped around her wasn't attacking her—it was shielding her with its own body. What kind of monster would do that? Kira tried to turn her head and see, but she couldn't. Dust, mud, and moss kept pressing into her face. And every time she moved her hands, someone tried to punch her face.

Suddenly, she heard a high-pitched whistle, and the mob quit. The monsters quickly backed away from Kira, all except for the one wrapped over her protectively. Someone began a slow clap. They shuffled, keeping their heads down. As the crowd parted, the clapper stepped forward to get a better look at the scene, no doubt.

Mr. Butt-Chin.

Kira tried to move, but there was a groan of pain above her. "Get off!" She grunted and tried to push herself off the ground. The weight rolled off of her and landed on the ground beside her.

The boy zeke. Just great! Now she would be indebted to him. Who knew? He might call in that debt the next time he got hungry. His face was swollen, and one eye was already turning purple. A pang of guilt rushed through her.

But she didn't ask for his help, didn't want it.

He looked to have taken a hefty punishment. His jeans were torn and his t-shirt had been shredded. A pool of red began forming under his back.

He was hurt worse than she had thought. She tried to reach over and touch his face, but his eyes opened. As she stared into the blackness, what she saw scared her. His eyes didn't look human. They had gone stark white, and silver flecks sparkled eerily in them. He turned those god-like eyes on Kira, and she skidded away from him.

Den approached Kira and circled her slowly, taking in the scene before him: the boy, Holly a few yards away, and the metal table leg that lay by her feet. Kira knew how bad this looked, but she'd done what she had to.

She studied him while he made sense of the situation. Den's black leather vest revealed strong, tattooed arms. Elegant script started at his hands and wrapped all the way around his arms and up to his neck. His red eyes seemed darker, more unpleasant today. Maybe because Kira had taken out one of his trainees.

Den shouted at a slave girl next to him. "Call Warrick, and get the zeke to the medical center. I need him recovered in time to compete in the next event."

Den turned angrily on the crowd of monsters. "What did you think you were doing?"

A large two-legged beast with long tusks coming out of his mouth stepped forward—a boar. Kira glanced at her arm and could see the distinct outline of a split-hoof impression. He was the obvious culprit.

The boar tried to speak, but the tusks seemed to impair his ability to enunciate. He squealed and then shape-shifted with a blur of skin and tusks, and a whiff of garlic. Suddenly, he was completely human-looking, although shorter. And less impressive to look at. No wonder so many of the monsters preferred their monster form or their half-shifted form. They were scarier. Kira couldn't ever imagine being scared of the short man with pimples.

"No one's ever stopped us from beating a slave before. Why now?" he asked.

"Because she's already been chosen," Den rebuked him.

"So as long as we don't kill it, can we still have fun with it? It does need to pay for killing Creeper, and for injuring Holly." The speaker was tall with spiky blond hair and black tips. He turned golden eyes on Kira, and she recognized him as the cheetah, Chaz. So this was his human form.

"Sorry to disappoint you, Chaz, but I think that would be a bad idea." Den turned and opened his arms wide, gesturing to everyone within hearing distance. "That goes for all of you. You are not allowed to harm her. If you have issues, you can take them up during training, but not before. Do you understand me?"

There were a few grumbles and complaints, but everyone seemed to get the picture. She was no longer fun if she couldn't be played with or harmed. Most of the crowd wandered off or went back to their rooms. Two large monsters carried Zeke off, probably toward the hospital wing.

"You know you didn't solve anything by that, right?" Den spoke directly to Kira, while nodding at Holly's body.

"I know," she answered softly. "I shouldn't have punched her." Kira looked down in mock submission, as Den paced around her. She knew how to pick her battles, and she'd had enough fighting for one day.

"Then why did you do it?" he asked.

"Because I wanted to," Kira answered smartly. "And I enjoyed it." She smiled and rubbed her knuckles, checking out the teeth imprints and skin that had been scraped off. She also felt a pang in her arm. A bruise was already forming along it from connecting with Holly's nunchucks.

Den grabbed Kira's arm. He felt along the bone, pressing hard, looking for a break. "The bone is bruised, not broken. You will live." He spoke in a clipped, uncaring tone. Just the way he said it rattled Kira's nerves.

"Obviously," Kira rolled her eyes sarcastically.

"I don't know how long if you can't control getting into fights. At this rate you won't survive long. I need to train you."

Kira's head snapped to attention. "I can take care of myself."

"Obviously," Den remarked, taking care to mimic her earlier response exactly.

"Why are you even going to the trouble to train me? I thought I was to be a slave."

"If that's what you want, I can still arrange it." Den yelled, pointing to the herd of monsters walking away. "It might almost be better. Life isn't sunshine and roses down here. You take what you get."

A ruckus came from one side of the room, and the monsters gathered around the screens eagerly.

"What's going on?" Kira asked.

"It seems that Hermes has scheduled the next event."

"Who's Hermes?"

"The game god."

"You mean like the mythical Greek god?"

Den stopped and gave her a *how-dumb-are-you?* stare. "Look around you, girl. There's no such thing as mythical. We're real." He pressed his hand to his chest. "The gods are real, although they've lost most of their mojo, but that doesn't mean that they are weak. They're still immortal. We call them Underlords now. All of this"—he gestured to the mixed races of slaves and monsters and back toward the city where the faint outline of the skyline could be seen—"exists for them. When humans no longer believed in the gods, they started to lose their power. That's why they chose to gather all of us mythical races, beasts, and fae and bring us here. So that they could rule over us. Because we know what it's like to not be believed in, we know what it's like to be forgotten."

"Can't you leave?"

"And go where? This is our world. This is our lot. We have more freedom here than we ever did in the upper lands." He turned away and focused on the screen.

"Except you're ruled by gods."

"And you're ruled by a president. What's the difference?"

"So these games, these events, are for what?"

"Hermes brought the Olympic Games back and merged it with the Roman games to appease the gods' restless nature. Otherwise Ares, our war god would become bored and wreak havoc among the races. Except these games are much bigger and…new rules." Den stopped walking and looked up at the screen. He seemed unimpressed. "Thousands of years of creativity at the hands of bored gods, not to mention their obsession with human sports, and this is what we get."

"Then why not stop the games? Why compete at all?"

"It's a balance. To keep peace upon the upper lands, we wage war through the games below. If that balance shifted, if the games ever stopped, all of them"—he pointed around to the monsters scattered throughout the room—"their purpose would cease. Most of our inherent nature is violent, so Ares is appeased when we turn it on each other. We're his own personal addiction." Den snarled.

"Each week it's different, always changing. So the owners will switch out their fighters and teams for different games. But that doesn't seem to be enough these days. They've added the random lottery, like a draft. Keeps the populace guessing and changes up the bets."

"You mean it's not always the same?"

"No, some events are more dangerous than others. And now they are sending non-fighters in at random to compete. It used to just be the criminals, then they added those that were in debt, then the slaves. Not anymore. Everyone has one of these bracers. If you're chosen, you go."

Now she was extremely interested in what was playing on the screen. She saw an attractive female with a pale face which slowly transitioned into pearlescent blue scales running down her neck and body. White hair fell past her shoulders. A red banner ran across the bottom of the broadcast, but Kira was unable to read the language.

The screen turned black, and words slowly appeared. Most around her cheered; a few groaned and shuffled away. She tried to read Den's expression and it didn't move an inch. "The next event is a gauntlet." Den's brow furrowed in worry.

"That doesn't sound bad."

"Believe me, it is."

"Then it would really suck to be chosen." Kira said rubbing her wrist under the band.

"Yeah, about that." He knocked his boots together and took a deep breath. "That's the reason your band is lit up."

Her head snapped, and she looked at him, "Say what?"

Den pointed at her band, and the white light that had been glowing there for hours. "You've been chosen. I have to make sure you show up for the gauntlet, or it'll be my head."

"This has been glowing for a while now. You're just telling me this?"

"I was busy."

She probably should have freaked out having never seen a gauntlet, but she'd watched tons of reality TV and sports. It couldn't possibly be that bad. Kira raised her chin. "Well, if I compete, I can win my freedom, right?"

"It's not that simple. There's a million to one odds that you could ever earn your freedom. And it would take years."

"Those are odds I can live by."

Den reached out and put pressure on her injury until she winced. He shook his head. "It's not what you think it is. It's worse. You're not getting a chance to compete and win. Those are odds you are going to die by."

NINE

"Run, girl!" Den shouted into her ear. At least it sounded like he was in her ear. In reality, he was a quite a few paces back.

Kira's side cramped, and she missed her timed jump onto the pile of scrap metal. She stumbled, tried to pull herself up, but a giant weight landed on her and flipped her onto her back. She looked up into the angry eyes of Den.

He mimed stabbing her in the heart with a fake knife. "Not good enough. You're dead again." She tried to sit up, but he shoved her in frustration, hard enough that her head bounced on the sheet metal. Butt-Chin ran his hands through his hair.

"Hey, I lasted longer that time." Kira painfully sat up and began to dust off her worn pants.

"Two minutes. You only lasted two minutes. Do you understand that the gauntlet is much longer? We don't have enough time. You're not even trying."

"Well, then why don't you train me with the others?"

"Ha! And let them know that you are their competition? Every single one of them would race in practice just to be the one to *accidentally* kill you." He kicked an old road sign. How did so much random garbage end up so far below the ground? "It's safer this way. But, I don't have enough resources to train you right."

Kira shrugged. "So I'll just train harder." She picked at a hangnail on the side of her thumb, purposely giving her thumb more attention than the white-blond Den. The angrier he was, the less she liked him. That was probably a good thing.

"You're lucky you are getting any training at all. I should just leave you to your own stubborn devices. Who knows, maybe you will survive on pure bull-headedness." He rubbed his forehead as if it pained him.

Kira's ears perked up at the backhanded compliment. She tried not to smile. Maybe she should be spending more effort, trying harder, training harder. But she didn't really see the point. She had kicked Holly's butt and killed Creeper. That made her pretty hard to kill in her book.

But it apparently wasn't enough for Den. Honestly, she thought it had more to do with Den being afraid she'd knock out her competition before the game.

Den turned to stare at her, his eyes filled with uncertainty, his lips a thin line. He shook his head. "I hate to do it, but it has to be done."

"What has to be done?"

"You don't fear for your life. You need to be scared to death. I'm going to have to find someone to beat some sense into you. Maybe the zeke—"

"Not bloody likely." Kira bristled at the mention of the zombie.

She didn't even see Den move, he was that fast. One moment he was three paces away, and the next he was right in front of her.

He grabbed her elbow and pulled her towards the door. "You listen to me. Down here you are the lowest on the food chain, not worth anyone's time or resources. You have skill, but you have no common sense. And right now, I can't teach you anything. So get back to your room."

She raised her lip in annoyance. "I'm not a child that you can just send to bed for not listening."

"That was not a suggestion. That was an order. Just be grateful I'm not beating you while I think of another way to train you." He shoved her off the pile of metal garbage where they stood, and she slid down the hill ungracefully.

Kira stood, shrugged, and started walking the path to the compound. No one could change her outlook.

Ten

Kira had found a way to pass the time by throwing rocks at an old outbuilding. Den hadn't trained her in two stinking days. She needed to do something—something loud and angry at the same time. She was working through a plan to try and escape when she saw a large equine beast out of the corner of her eye. Kira stiffened.

Warrick.

His beady eyes stared at her accusingly. "Your recklessness has caused a lot of damage."

Kira dropped the rock and looked at him. "She deserved it! Holly was trying to kill me. I was only defending myself." Kira swore at herself when she realized she'd been goaded into talking to the beast. She had made a silent vow to never speak to the betrayer again.

"I'm not talking about the hedge witch. I'm talking about the zeke." There was a moment of awkwardness as Kira realized her mistake.

"Oh, well, um. I didn't do that. He did that himself."

Warrick stepped forward, and Kira moved backwards. "He was injured protecting you."

"Hey, I never asked him to. He should have let well enough alone. Then he wouldn't have been injured."

Warrick stomped his hoof. "You don't get it, do you? Those injuries would have killed a human. They almost killed the zeke. It's a good thing he didn't leave well enough alone, otherwise you would have been dead." Warrick pointed his tan finger at Kira.

"Haven't you heard, ol' man? I'm already dead!" Kira swatted the finger away irritably.

The centaur's eyes softened. "I know you were chosen. And your first event is the gauntlet."

Kira looked away from him and stared at the blinking exit sign down the hall. She swallowed and nodded slowly.

"Come with me, girl."

Warrick took her to another wing of the compound, to a black gate. He punched a code and the gate opened.

A surge of excitement raced through Kira's body. Was he letting her go? She could finally leave and try and escape. The moment lasted only that, a *moment*, before she looked down at her bracer. She'd never truly escape until she found a way to get this off of her. Even though her heart was ready to run her feet didn't move.

Warrick must have read her mind. "I have permission to take you out into the city. You wouldn't make it very far without me anyway." Warrick held the gate open and waited for Kira to pass through. When it was securely locked again, he started down a tunnel.

So the waterway wasn't the only way to get back to the city. She'd come from the city by boat to Remus's home; now they were heading a different way. But not a way she'd remember in the near future. Every time the path came to a T, Warrick turned a different direction. There were no markings other than some form of ancient Greek-looking script scribbled on the wall. Even with her memory, it would take numerous trips by the same route for her to figure her way to the city.

But then what? What would she do? She would be even more in danger in a city surrounded by monsters. The memory of an animal feeding outside the Gamblers' Market made her shudder and feel a little sick. She wouldn't know how to traverse the waterways to make it back to the surface. It wasn't like there were ladders and manhole covers to the surface every hundred yards or so.

From what she'd overheard, they were miles underground, and every entrance into the city and the surrounding area was guarded night and day by monsters similar to Nessie. Her only chance of survival was to stay here long enough to learn how to get out. Even if it meant pretending to forgive the stupid centaur and playing at being nice. She could do that, she guessed. It seemed to be working so far, because he was taking her out of Remus's for a bit.

Now whether or not she should be thankful for that was another matter. She would wait to see if whatever surprise Warrick had in store was a blessing or a curse. Her legs were burning with exertion when she saw the tunnel begin to get lighter with colored neons. They were definitely getting near the city.

"Stay close. Don't wander off. There are things walking around in daylight that are more dangerous than your worst nightmare."

"Don't worry. I'm not stupid. But if this is some sort of trap, I'm telling you in advance that it's every *girl* for herself."

Warrick turned and raised an eyebrow at her. His lip curled in silent laughter when he caught her nuance on the world girl and not man or centaur. "Duly noted and expected."

When they hit the hub of the city, Kira was once again amazed by the beauty and the structure of the buildings. This time, since she wasn't fearing for her life and future, she had the time to take in her surroundings and try to memorize markers.

She stared at a beautiful naturally-formed column thousands of feet in diameter that rose up in the middle of the city. It glittered and reflected the colors around it. When they moved, she noticed that it didn't just glitter from lights, she was seeing the reflection of windows.

The column was a fortress of sorts.

"What's that?" she pointed at the beautiful formation.

"Olympus Tower."

"I bet you I know who lives there." Kira said. "The gods."

"The Underlords, yes. They live there, and anyone rich enough to be invited lives there. Freedom tokens can buy you anything here."

As they traveled, Kira couldn't help but notice the beauty and cleanliness of the tower complex compared to the decline of the rest of the civilization. It seemed to mirror what was happening above in her own world. The rich staying rich while the poor were fighting for food.

They turned down an alley and disturbed a large animal eating out of the dumpster. The creature stood three feet tall and hissed at them angrily. Clawed hands darted out of a faded gray army jacket and swung at them threateningly. "Mine, mine!" it growled. "I found it first." The beast moved like lightning and jumped onto the trash can, kneeling over its prize of rotting food.

Warrick stomped his hooves and his tail whipped with tension. "Keep your trash. We are only interested in passing through."

The alley beast didn't seem to register Warrick's words and still jumped up and down angrily. His teeth gnashed in challenge like a starving stray dog. When the centaur tried to pass him, the animal pounced and dug his claws into Warrick's back. Warrick screamed in anger and tried to buck the creature off.

Kira grabbed a stray plank of wood and swung it at the beast's head. It saw the threat and jumped off of Warrick, nimbly attaching itself to a sign hanging from a building. She'd only missed by inches. It screeched its hatred at Kira, and she was about to try and attack it again, but Warrick stopped her.

"Come, he isn't worth your time. Even our poor must eat, and they too must fight for their right to survive. We don't need to give him a battle over scraps." Warrick's voice held a hint of aching sadness.

Kira couldn't help but begin to respect him—just a little. His wise words resonated in her soul. Seconds before, he'd been attacked for trying to walk through an alley, his back laced with wounds that bled freely and mixed with his equine coat. Yet he still spoke of understanding and tolerance for those less fortunate than himself.

Where were people like Warrick in Portland when she'd been the one eating out of trash cans? If only humans had a scrap of the centaur's dignity, the whole race would be better off.

They walked for another quarter mile, various beings watching them from behind closed doors. At one point, Kira thought for sure she had seen Grater in the distance with a chain around another slave for the slave market. Was it in that direction? How anyone could tell north or south without the sun was beyond her, but maybe after living here long enough you just knew.

When they came to a dead end, Kira began to worry that maybe she really had made the wrong decision. A figure moved away from the wall and stepped in front of them. A long, dark cloak hid his features.

***

Den watched them approach and felt a moment's hesitation again. What was he going to do with her? He liked her spirit and wanted to stick it to Remus. The best way to get revenge was to make sure she made it through the next gauntlet. Then he'd figure something out. With Remus's threat fresh in his mind though, he needed to do something drastic now. Something that would make her take this seriously. Like scare her.

"Thanks, Warrick, for bringing her." Den kept his voice to a whisper. He reached to grab Kira's arm, but she backed away into Warrick.

The centaur didn't budge. "You can't be trained until you've seen a game in action," he said. "Most of us have grown up either fearing the games or secretly being fascinated with them."

"I worked my tail off doing what Den wanted me to do. Maybe it's him. Maybe he's a lousy trainer."

"And yet, I'm the only one you're going to get," Den spoke without looking at her.

"What? No really?" she said.

Den ignored her sarcasm and walked to a brick wall with an electric voice box sticking out of it about chest-high. He pushed the red button.

A few moments later, a high pitched voice answered. "Hello?"

"Ferb, it's Den and Warrick." Static followed, and Den inwardly cussed and wondered briefly if he owed Ferb any money. He owed a lot of money to a lot of people.

"You brought Rick? It's been ages since I've seen that quadruped donkey bait of a face." The excited reply sounded like a string of gibberish, and Den breathed a sigh of relief, which was cut short. "Den, don't think I've forgotten our wager."

Den racked his brain. What did—?

"You owe me a pint at Shady's. What brings you to the archives? Think of putting down another bet?"

Oh good, it was only a pint he owed. He needed to keep it at that. "Not this time, Ferb. I've got a newbie that needs your expertise—never seen the games. Thought you would like to show her the ropes. Maybe show her a past gauntlet."

The call box buzzed and, across the alley, a black gate swung open. Warrick motioned for Kira to enter the passageway first. There was hardly any room—the passageway was barely big enough to squeeze her in front of Warrick's huge body, but all three of them managed somehow. The gate swung closed, and a motor whirred above them. As the cage trembled and descended into the ground, she pinched herself to keep from calling out in fear. When the elevator stopped, it opened into a huge room filled with fluorescent light.

He had to blink to adjust to the sudden brightness.

The gate opened. Den and Warrick stepped out and immediately moved to the middle of the room towards Ferb. He scurried over and greeted them.

While they chatted for a moment, Den watched Kira study the room. TV screens lined three walls, including digital projection screens and even a wall of water.

Everywhere flashed images of events from the gauntlet. People running for their lives, killing each other, setting traps. Other screens showed the aftermath, a smiling champion getting interviewed. One wall was covered with pictures of the top ranked champions of all time. Creeper's picture was on the wall with a 4 under his frame.

Ferb's long tail and ears twitched with excitement when Warrick introduced her. "I'm very pleased to meet you. No one's ever brought me a human to teach before." His nose twitched, and he offered his small hand.

Kira shook it gingerly with two fingers and Den snorted.

"Pleased to meet you. I'm glad to be here." She was able to paste on a fake smile.

Den was amused at her obvious awkwardness when confronted with Ferb. Yes, he was short and fuzzy, but also very deadly. Den hoped she was smart enough to get past the cuddly exterior and realize that he'd brought her to The Expert on the games.

***

Wow, this place. Kira studied their host again. He looked like an oversized meerkat with a tail and eyes so large they could only be described as boggly. He was super cute. But the décor suggested he had a dark fascination.

Not cuddly.

Kira glanced back at the picture of Creeper on the wall. She felt zero remorse when she looked at his gaunt skin and haunting smile.

Warrick was distracted by a large screen with a large ogre-looking beast tearing through a crowd of people with ease. He picked one up and threw him to the ground with ease and then began to stomp on him crudely before running. The camera seemed to love him—the crowd favorite.

Appalled but unable to look away, Kira stepped closer to the screen and stared, mesmerized by the destruction and chaos left in the monster's wake. This was where she would have to fight to survive?

A large obstacle course filled with deadly looking pitfalls, acid rivers, and traps. Some guy tried to swing over the river of acid and got knocked off his rope by the whitish beast. He fell into acid, but the death wasn't swift. It was horribly loud and painful—Kira had to turn away. Just as she looked back, the camera zoomed in on the monster's final moments. Kira's stomach heaved. The crowd went wild, screaming and whistling. Only a few onlookers groaned and shook their heads in defeat.

The perpetrator who knocked him off took center screen, and a score box appeared below his face. Bogeyman's bio, weight, and other stats were listed. This horrible looking boggart weighed nearly three hundred pounds. Of the seven races he'd run, he'd won five. A few seconds later, a gold box appeared with numbers in the shape of bones.

The tally was twenty-one.

"What does that mean?" Kira had to be sure. Maybe the number didn't mean what she thought it did.

Ferb scooted over on a chair with wheels; he looked up at the screen and grinned. "Ah, the kill tally. It helps the betting. Plus, the higher the number usually means the more popular you are."

"That's disgusting!"

"Only to you. Here, it's the same as seeing a baseball player's RBI's. It's an integral part of our life. Soon you will have one too, if I understand correctly."

Ferb pushed off from the table and flew across the room, still holding onto the office chair. The chair slid and slowed down by a long display of cases and frames.

Kira followed at a slower pace. He waved her over impatiently and pointed into a glass case. When she leaned down to focus, she gasped at the objects inside. There was a bloody shoe, a torn uniform, and various other objects.

"You see that?" He pointed excitedly. "That was the shoe worn by Zephyr in the 1507 Championships. And that was the uniform of Tora in the '13 semifinals; she was the favorite, but a dragon obliterated her three yards from the finish line. I had to search long and hard for that—traded a years' worth of tokens for it." He spouted off facts and information about every item in his case. His warm breath left small steam circles everywhere.

"But no one has been able to beat the Labyrinth. I think that's why the Underlords are picking more chosens."

He'd almost managed to get her interested, but a small object on a plush purple pillow caught her eye. Once she recognized the object as a mummified finger she turned and ran for the door.

Warrick blocked her way.

She ran right into him and started hitting him with her fists. "Why would you bring me here? Get me out!"

Warrick let her pound him with her fists, sighing. "We thought it best that you understood what you were getting yourself into. You need to be prepared."

"And this was the best way? To show me videos and body parts of past contestants. Are you nuts?" Kira wiped her tears on her jacket sleeve and stepped away. She kept her back to the TV screens that replayed the best kills of the centuries and found the one spot in the room that didn't have anything dead or dying displayed on it. She focused on the framed picture of a young Ferb waving a flag at a race. He was truly a lifelong collector of the games' artifacts.

"I want to leave…now!"

"Not yet," Den argued. "We brought you here so you can watch old events and see what you are up against. Ferb knows everything there is to know about the past and *current* champions. He can tell you their weaknesses and strengths. He's able to find out things about the courses that no one else knows. He is your biggest asset, when you have nothing else."

"Are you trying to say I'm weak?" Kira argued.

"No, I'm saying you're human." As he walked towards Kira, she backed up. "So you are going to sit here, listen, and learn."

"Why do you care?"

Warrick spoke up. He looked at her, emotion splayed across his face—dignity, sorrow, and compassion. "Because," he let out a breath slowly and looked at Den. "Not all of us are heartless monsters."

Kira felt something soft brush against the back of her knees, and she fell onto the seat of the chair that Ferb had vacated seconds before. He crawled up onto her shoulder, and Den pushed her in front of the largest screen imaginable.

Ferb held the remote control. He began playing through years of tapes and droning on about the rules of the game. He would grab her head when he wanted her to pay attention to a small detail, and she quickly learned what a valuable asset he was. He didn't miss a thing.

Kira made it three minutes before she started to puke.

Warrick already had a bucket on hand and deftly slipped it in front of her. Ferb just patted her head and rewound the scene again. "You missed it; this is where a machine called the eliminator is hidden—usually in the second leg. If you aren't careful, it'll chop off your head." He said it so nonchalantly that Kira tried very carefully not to heave again, but to concentrate on the scene. If Ferb was going to make her watch every scene she missed because she was otherwise engaged, then she had better do her best to catch it the first time around.

It didn't work. Kira emptied her stomach three more times before the day was over, and then she passed out sometime during the last leg of the championship. Apparently there were various events. Then each quarter there were separate mini-games the runners entered before the playoffs—the semifinals and finally the Labyrinth.

First up was the gauntlet: a type of obstacle course where runners were released in teams. The goal was to try and make it to the finish line with as many team members intact as possible. There were many courses just to keep things fresh. The gauntlet was apparently one of the more popular games in the circuit.

She learned that there were underground games called the ring and monsterball. But for her, for today, Ferb focused on how the gauntlet worked, and the jobs of the runners. Clearly, no one thought she would survive to compete in the Labyrinth, so she wisely kept her mouth shut.

***

Kira looked exhausted by the time they made it back to the compound. And her mood reflected that clearly. Den had stayed in the city and asked Warrick to escort her back. She had been quiet, lost in her inner thoughts, clearly disturbed by what she'd seen.

"There's one more stop I'd like you to make with me." Warrick turned and entered the infirmary wing. His tail swished behind him, and when he opened the door, he inhaled deeply of the mingling scents of disinfectant and cloves. Kira followed him into the infirmary, but she kept to the edge of the room.

He tried to picture this familiar place through her eyes. He'd tried to spruce up the sterile environment with potted plants that he'd found. A large metal table stood off to one side. While it was similar to the one in his home, due to the size of his patients, this one was twice as large. There were glass cabinets with various medicines, ointments, and salves, but nothing threatening. No mangled body parts or torture devices. Just a hallway that led to the operating room and the recovery rooms.

He headed back toward those now. Kira followed and he paused in front of his destination, listening carefully to the healing occupant on the other side. There were no sounds of distress. It would be safe for her.

The boy had sacrificed so much to help Kira, but Warrick had a feeling there was more to it than that. Warrick suspected their fates were somehow intertwined. Maybe they just needed another nudge. He was more than capable of offering that.

He handed Kira a small pouch. "Here. You need to start making more friends and less enemies."

She took the pouch from him and eyed the door warily. Warrick opened the door and physically pushed her into the room.

Kira stiffened and pushed against him, but she was no match for his strength. With another swift nudge, he propelled her into the room.

***

The door closed with a click. Warrick peeked through the glass pane and motioned with his hands for her to move forward.

A thin blue curtain separated her from the room, and the shadow of someone or something moved behind it. The smell of disinfectant and the sterile décor brought back unwanted memories of trips to the hospital with her mother. Of sitting idly by, while her mother spun outrageous lies about how she got her injuries. Whether it was tripping down a flight of stairs or falling out of a tree, the lies came smoothly. The nurses barely blinked at Ellie's excuses, and the whole time Kira hoped they would challenge her mother, ask if she lived with an abusive husband. No one bothered, no one cared, and so Kira kept silent, living with the abuse.

But she wasn't that little girl anymore. She could take care of herself.

Gathering her courage, Kira gripped the pouch Warrick had given her. She didn't know what it was or what to do with it, but she wasn't alone. And she needed to know whose room she'd invaded. She moved forward and pulled the curtain to the side. The sight of a half-naked person took her aback.

The zeke boy stood there wearing only a pair of denim jeans, his muscular torso bare. Kira felt her cheeks begin to burn bright red, and she stammered and tried to look elsewhere, to look anywhere except for his sculpted body. Why, oh, why couldn't he have had an ugly body? Isn't that how zombies should look? Ugly, gaunt and thin. No, his skin was smooth and heavily muscled. Kira's mouth actually went dry, but Zeke pretended to not see her. Either that or he really didn't care.

He turned his back to her as he grabbed a blue t-shirt draped across a nearby chair. Deep gashes, angry welts, purple bruises marred his entire back. From protecting her. The realization stole her breath.

***

Zeke heard her enter. He actually smelled her when she was out in the hall, and the scent, the aroma of her skin alone was enough to drive him wild. He had to get control of himself, of his hunger. She stepped around the curtain when she saw him and stared at his muscular chest. Her face flushed red in embarrassment. He liked that he could affect her like that.

Proof that he affected her as much as she affected him. He pretended to ignore her as he reached for his shirt. He heard her intake of breath at seeing his back.

He turned on her, livid, at the gasp. Pity. Did she pity him? His anger rushed to the surface, and he began to lose grip on his control. He tossed the shirt onto the bed and stepped towards her.

She shook under his furious and hungry gaze. Good. Because he should be feared and not pitied.

Zeke crossed to her in two quick paces, and his large hands reached for her throat. As his thumbs brushed her collarbone, an electric warning sent a shock through his blood. She jumped. Had she felt it too? With his hands around her throat he could feel her pulse against his thumbs. He wanted to press his lips against the same spot and feel her heartbeat with his mouth.

"Wait!" She thrust up the leather pouch between their bodies, using it as a shield. "Here, it's for you." She pushed the pouch directly into his face and he backed off. His hands brushed her forearms as he moved away. The tingling sensation stopped, and he felt himself begin to calm.

He looked at the pouch quizzically, and his gaze swayed back to Kira's. She was tense, but not fearful. He glanced at the mirror in the room. His eyes were still white, but they no longer held a dangerous gleam to them. So, she wasn't forgetting what she'd seen mere seconds ago, but she was still wary.

Maybe she had felt the same thing when they touched. Interesting. But he couldn't let it happen again. He almost lost himself. He almost bit her. He needed to scare her. To keep her away.

When he didn't move to take the pouch, she tossed it onto his bed and moved towards the door. The farther away she moved, the braver she became. Almost to the door, she turned, head high. Her hair swung in its long ponytail as she looked back over her shoulder. "You shouldn't have done what you did the other day. But for what it's worth, thanks."

***

The zeke boy didn't move. His hands were clenched by his sides. His chest heaved with deep breaths.

Was that for show? Did zekes actually breathe? There were so many things she had yet to learn.

"You're *not* welcome." She didn't need an education to read the bitterness in his voice. He looked at her through heavy lidded eyes, challenging her, daring her to come near him again.

Kira's eyes widened for only a second, but she recovered in record time. "Good!" she retorted snidely. "Then I won't feel obligated to return the favor. *Ever*!" Kira slammed the door and entered the hallway. Her heart raced with adrenaline. Her hands were still shaking, but she wasn't sure if it was from fear, hate, or the sight of his bare chest. Kira caught the sound of laughter coming from behind the door.

Kira's rage returned, and she had to catch herself from screaming back a retort that would make her mother cringe. She was about to push the door open and punch him in the mouth when she noticed Warrick's silhouette down the hall, waiting for her.

Grinding her teeth, she met him halfway.

"Done?" he asked.

"Yeah, sure," she quipped.

"Did you give it to him? Did he like it?"

"Uh yeah, it was awesome! Best gift e-v-e-r." Kira answered uncomfortably. She was now too embarrassed to ask about what was in the pouch, for fear of being caught in a lie. Maybe it was better if she didn't know anyway. Warrick looked at her slyly; he could sense her lie. But instead of confronting her about it, he ignored it.

Eleven

After leaving Warrick and Zeke everything had been a bit of a blur. Since then, Kira had simply sat and rocked herself in silence. It was the only thing that seemed to calm her nerves. When she let everything that happened soak in, when she really pondered it all, it hit her. She was a goner; she knew the odds of surviving.

She had absolutely zero chance.

Kira sat paralyzed with fear in her room for two days.

She ignored anyone who knocked and pushed a chair in front of the door, but it offered zero protection. If a monster wanted into her room bad enough, it would break down the door. Still, the chair gave her at least the illusion of safety. But that's all this was, an illusion.

She had deluded herself into thinking she could survive among the monsters. She had seen the tapes. She wished that she had never followed Warrick, and she wished she had never sat and watched the race, but she had. There was no turning back. She couldn't erase what she had seen.

The slight sound of metal scraping across the floor was all the notice Kira had. On instinct, she rolled off her bunk and landed on the floor, missing the knife that sunk into her mattress by mere inches. Her room was pitch black, so she had to rely on her hearing.

Someone swore quietly and pulled the knife out of the mattress. Her only advantage was that *they* couldn't see in her darkened room either. Probably. She lifted her mattress, knocked it over, shoved it into her attacker, and ran for the door. Her feet sounded loud even to her own ears, the thud thud thud of her boots as she darted toward freedom. Clawed hands raked across her shoulder. She cried out at the stinging pain, but she spun and flung her body at the door and it burst open into the hallway.

Too close. Too similar. Tears fell down her cheeks as she fled the attacker. She was running just as hard from her memory.

She had just turned fifteen, when Bernie really started to notice her. She installed a lock on her bedroom door and slept with her dad's combat knife under her pillow, but it wasn't long before Bernie broke through her bedroom door while her mom was passed out downstairs on the couch.

When her dad had taught Kira how to defend herself as a child, she never imagined she would be using those techniques to defend herself from her own stepfather. It was over with quickly. Bernie was drunk and stumbling into the dresser when he came for her. She tried to threaten him, but he charged.

She stabbed him in the shoulder. His howl of pain rang in her ears as she pushed him away, grabbed her backpack, and jumped out the window. She didn't care if he died, but she knew, more than likely he would survive.

Thankfully, Kira had been prepared. She'd filled her pack with cash she had stolen in small increments from their savings jar, a change of clothes, trail mix, and a jacket. She was still in her pajamas when she shimmied down the drain pipe and ran down the street barefoot. She never looked back, not for one moment. Not even to turn back for her mom.

And here she was all over again, running, not looking back. She ran down the hallway, down the stairs, and away from whatever was in her room. She was looking up the stairwell as she ran down, trying to see if someone or something was still in pursuit.

That's how she crashed into the person coming up the stairs.

"Kira. What's wrong?" Zeke's arms flew up to catch her as she started to tumble to the ground.

"S-someone tried to kill me...in my room…while I was s-sleeping."

Zeke's eyes darkened as he studied the stairwell. A barely discernable shadow two floors up moved, and all that followed was the soft click of a metal door closing. Her pursuer had retreated. Zeke pulled his hand away from Kira's shoulder. Blood coated his palm. His eyes went wide with hunger.

The double doors beside them opened, and Den rushed in from outside. Zeke quickly handed Kira over and took off—after her attacker or away from her. She wasn't sure.

"Are you okay?" Den eyed her bleeding shoulder.

She pulled away from him and watched him warily. "Yes, it's just a cut. Someone tried to attack me. Zeke, he went after them." She pointed up the stairwell. "I think—"

"He'll be fine. He can handle himself." He spun her around and inspected her wound more carefully. "For now you have a bigger problem."

"What?"

"It's time."

"What do you mean?"

"The truck is here. It's time to send our champions and the chosen."

Twelve

"Don't show fear. Don't make yourself a target. If you present yourself as weak, the bigger mobs will try to kill you during the race, purely to up their kill tally. It's all about the numbers." Den tried to coach her as they walked toward a large truck sent by the Underlords to collect the competitors. He had given her a rag, and she shoved it in her jacket over her shoulder to staunch the blood flow. It sure didn't help the pain, but there wouldn't be time to see Warrick.

Two guards stood on each side of the truck with a tablet that told them who to collect from the facility.

"There's two that have been selected from this gym." The guard on the left called out to the crowd. "You must present yourself. Now!"

"I can't do it." Heat flooded Kira. She saw the armed guards and stopped, tried to pull away out of Den's grasp, but it was too strong. "I don't want to die."

"You have to go. I've sent you help. You just have to trust me," Den growled into her ear. "Now stand up and make me proud. Show them, Kira, what you're made of."

"Uh, meat and witty sarcasm." There it went, her odd humor that popped up whenever she was scared, her crazy defense mechanism.

"Well, I think most would like at least one of those attributes." At least he was trying to help ease the tension.

"The chosen will present themselves now!" The guard took out his gun and was about to fire it into the crowd when Kira separated herself from the monsters.

"I'm here." She walked forward, shoulders back, head lifted high. She held up her white blinking band, and they scanned it before nodding for her to get into the truck bed. She looked back to her trainer out of the corner of her eyes. A sad sigh escaped his thin lips. His body language said he didn't think she was going to come back alive.

The two guards snickered and shuffled from side to side. If Kira wasn't already in pain from her shoulder, she probably would have thought of another witty comeback, but all she had the energy to do was glare back at his butt-chin in anger.

Everyone—runners, slaves, trainers, and even Warrick—had gathered outside as they waited for the other chosen to appear. There was a long buzzing noise that resounded through the compound, and a few minutes later, the doors to one of the buildings opened.

A tall, slim man wearing an Aerosmith t-shirt strode out cheering loudly. The crowd yelled and patted his back. Kira recognized Chaz's dark-tipped hair as he turned and pumped his fists at the crowd. He leapt into the air and the truck shook under his weight. He waved and ducked under the frame. Then he plunked down on the bench and held out his wrist with a grin.

The guard scanned Chaz's white blinking band. He was the other chosen.

When he saw her, his smile disappeared. He raised his lips and let out a low growl that could be felt through the floor of the truck. A moment later, he plastered his smile back on and returned to playing the crowd.

They chanted his name over and over like he was their idol. Maybe now that Creeper was dead, he'd become the crowd's favorite.

"Now it's time for open enrollment." The guard with the tablet swept his hand toward the truck. "You'll be paid for entering."

Kira couldn't help but feel that the whole selection process was similar to cattle being loaded on a truck and sent to slaughter. A few shoved each other towards the truck, but it didn't seem like any were serious.

And then, two other volunteers appeared from among the milling monsters and hesitantly entered the truck. One was a tall willowy man, the other an Amazonian woman wearing leather armor. Each of their bands were loaded with tokens for volunteering.

When no one else came forward, one of the guards climbed in the back with them, and the other closed the truck bed and headed for the driver's seat.

The double doors of the gym opened again and, with little fanfare, a single figure walked out. There was no convoy of aggressive fans or well-wishers following him. The crowd did quit whistling long enough to part in surprise as the zeke headed toward the truck. The group whispered among themselves.

He jumped into the truck bed and didn't look at her. There was something on the side of his mouth, and his eyes didn't look as feral as they did a few moments ago. But that didn't mean he found the attacker. With the way he was ignoring her, she'd guess no.

As the engine roared to life, the crowd began screaming again and wishing everyone luck. A tug at the back of Kira's jacket made her turn around in surprise.

An older man with unbelievably bright blue hair and blue eyes spoke to her through the slats. "I'm betting on you to finish the race." She tried to raise her head to see more of him, so she could remember him, but he disappeared into the crowd.

It was singlehandedly the nicest thing anyone had said or done for her. Just that comment made her believe in herself, because someone else believed in her. She tried to remember if she had ever seen the man with blue hair and couldn't place him.

"To the Crystal Gorge," the driver said. "I got to sit front row once, and got christened with the remains of some loser. Nice, eh?"

The other guard grunted his approval. "Feel like it gave ya good luck?"

"Yeah, yeah."

The Crystal Gorge was, a fan favorite, Ferb had said, because something so beautiful had been turned into something so deadly. What else had he told her?

The guards' dry laughter made her skin crawl, especially when the driver kept looking through the rearview mirror directly at her. She shifted her eyes and stared at her feet, which only caused him to laugh louder.

No one spoke in the truck bed. Once the crowd was gone, the reality of their future was upon the runners. False bravado and fake smiles deserted them, replaced by a few coughs and an awkward silence. Even the exuberant Chaz's mood mellowed in the seriousness of the situation. He rested his head on his knees and actually seemed to be sleeping. If only she could figure out how to do that.

She would have tried to make conversation with the woman warrior but decided it was better to distance herself from her. It would be easier to not know someone's name if they were going to be dead in a few hours. Was that being heartless? Kira didn't think so. It felt practical.

Something tickled her collarbone, and she reached up. Her fingers came away wet with blood. It didn't hurt anymore, but she must have jostled the wound. She tried to hide and wipe off the blood but was unsuccessful. Three hungry pairs of eyes stared at her, as if the blood were an aromatic perfume. The willowy man actually licked his lips. Chaz lifted his head from his knees and studied her through squinted eyes. Zeke's eyes were the most calculating of all—void of emotion.

Kira had to wonder what would possess any of the last three to volunteer for the race. Did they need the money? Were they in debt? Or was it for the glory? Reluctantly, she tried to focus on the coming race.

She needed to settle her stomach and nerves, to remember everything Ferb said about Crystal Gorge. After all, he'd made her watch a video of the last gauntlet held there. Obviously, crystal was the theme. Many traps and roadblocks were made out of the beautiful but deadly crystal. There were hidden pitfalls filled with dagger-sharp crystal, a trek up a sharpened crystal mountain, and what else? Her mind drew a blank, and she groaned in frustration. She never would have believed that she would be thanking Warrick for making her watch all of those videos. They may be her only hope of survival.

Moments later, the truck slowed as it passed through the gates into a valley filled with brightly colored tents and small outbuildings. There, guards carried no guns. But then again, none were needed when your weapon was large teeth and you sported claws capable of ripping someone to shreds.

Kira had been expecting cages, similar to Grater's courtyard. She was surprised when women floated out of a building wearing silk translucent dresses. No wait, the dresses weren't translucent—the girls were. They surrounded each of the trucks and waited as the back gate was lowered and each of the runners stepped down onto the stone pavement. The ghost-like apparitions separated and stood by each runner waiting patiently.

Kira hung back and watched as Chaz followed the ghost girl almost eagerly, followed by the willowy man, and the warrior woman, and finally the zeke. When the courtyard was empty accept for Kira and her ghostly escort, she slowly followed what she assumed was her specter into the building.

The scene inside could only have been described as fattening the pig for a slaughter. Her specter led her into a room with sterile white furniture and tables. Chaz was reclining on an off-white couch, eating from a huge array of food laid out on clear glass trays and plates. Zeke stood by a window looking outside of the building.

A flat screen TV hung on the main wall, and it played announcements and promoted the upcoming race—scheduled for a few hours from now.

On the screen, two warlocks bickered back and forth on who they thought would win today's race.

***

Remus ignored the commentators as he waited in the sponsors' box for his precious cargo. Howl should have been here an hour ago. Remus didn't like to be kept waiting.

Ssirone walked in and made himself comfortable in the large chair by the window, the perfect spot to wait and watch the games. "There'sss a rumor that you entered a human girl." He turned to look at Remus, a smug smile on his snake-like face.

"She was drafted," Remus snarled, "and I wouldn't worry about her much longer."

"Too bad ssshe wassssn't drafted before ssshe killed your zeke," Ssirone said.

Remus wanted to comment, but his bracer beeped and a message came across the screen.

They were here. Finally, a boggart.

Moments later, Howl, a muscular man with gray hair, came into the room leading a boggart as large as an ogre in chains. The thing had pale white flesh with reddish eyes and very sharp teeth. A killing machine. Just not against him.

"You're late," Remus said, while trying to hide his pleasure at the retaining the new fighter.

"You're early," Howl countered and pulled on the chain. The boggart went wild and leapt forward to attack Remus, his mouth snapping, and claws aimed at his throat. Howl pulled back on the chain with inches to spare.

"Oh ho! I like that," Remus cheered at Bogeyman's attempt to kill him. "Such a killing instinct. Does he take orders?"

"Only if they are to kill." Howl's muscles bunched as he strained to keep the boggart under control.

Ssirone had obviously not liked the fact that there was a feral runner in the room, because he quickly exited out a side door.

"Leave us," Remus commanded. He waved at Howl who looked unsure. "Drop his chain and go! I don't need you anymore."

Howl snarled, wolf-like. "Your neck, not mine." He released the boggart's chain and left the same way he came.

Remus stepped in front of the white malformed man-beast and looked into those hate-filled eyes. "Listen here. I own you. You kill for me now."

The boggart's white eyes turned to focus on Remus's voice. He wasn't sure how much the beast understood. Boggarts weren't known for their speaking abilities.

"I'll make it worth your while," Remus held up his bracer, but the boggart shook his head. "I know your kind. I know what you want. You don't want freedom tokens. You like the events, you like the killing. I do too. It's much more interesting when runners believe they have a chance."

The boggart opened his mouth wide, revealing rows of teeth in what Remus assumed was a smile. "I'll tell you what. You kill for me, and I'll kill your old master, Howl. How does that sound?"

Bogeyman's mouth opened and his lips moved oddly as he tried to speak. "I kill girl, I kill you."

Remus laughed. "You can try. But you don't know what kind of monster you're dealing with." His hand reached out and he grasped Bogeyman's bald head. "I'm a boggart's worst nightmare." Bogeyman's white eyes rolled back into his head in pain as Remus unleashed his power, slowly melting the edges of the mind. If he did enough, he could melt the entire brain. But he needed the boggart to obey.

The beast whimpered, "You're a Banthor."

"You kill for me," Remus repeated again.

"I kill for you." Bogeyman ground out between his teeth.

***

A white ogre-looking monster popped up on the screen, and Kira recognized Bogeyman. The warlock called Zephyr was counting on Bogeyman to win and also take down at least ten runners with him.

Chaz hissed at the TV and threw whatever food he had been eating at the screen. It landed with a soft thud, and the brown pudding-like mixture stuck to Zephyr's face and then slowly eked down, obscuring most of the warlock's expression.

Was this the same Zephyr Ferb had mentioned? From the 1509 championships? If it was—she did the math—he was five hundred years old. After a few minutes she learned it was indeed the same Zephyr, a Paladin now. How many years had it taken him to earn his freedom?

She was so preoccupied with the TV that Kira didn't feel the gentle tug on her sleeve as the ghost tried to undress her. "Hey! I don't think so."

The ghost tried to pull on her shirt a few more times but she swatted the ethereal hand away. Or what she thought was her hand. Kira grabbed ahold of her shirt and refused to let go, for fear it could disappear at any moment. She glanced up to see that the two other ghosts were dressing Chaz and Zeke. Kira turned around abruptly. What? Did no one believe in privacy?

The girl seemed determined to get Kira dressed, but when another tug came at her pants, she screamed and pushed at the ghost. A small noise escaped the being. "All right, but I'm not undressing. If you want me to wear the stupid clothes then they need to go over what I'm wearing now. Do you understand?"

The ghost solidified enough that she could see the girl smile widely and gesture towards a side door. It opened, and the werewolf from her compound and a black snake-like being entered the room wearing uniforms. Kira took the stack of clothes from the specter and exited the door the two runners had just come from. There wasn't any signage, signifying whether it was boy girl specific, so she just pressed on through. It was a stark and utilitarian shower and changing room. Kira's cheeks burned red at the thought of how close to being humiliated she was.

Regaining her composure, she looked for a shower closest to the door, so—if she had to—she could make a quick escape. Stripping quickly and pulling the knife out of her boot, Kira entered the shower stall and closed the tattered curtain. Fiddling with the knobs produced a wonderful stream of hot water, much to Kira's delight. She did the best she could to clean herself with a knife in her hand and keep her wounded shoulder turned away from the water. She needed to let it be as much as possible.

Warrick's magical drops of healing would've been great right about then.

Over the spray of the shower, she heard the locker room door open. Footsteps entered.

Kira gripped the knife close to her body, ready to spring at the curtain if it so much as moved.

Nothing. The footsteps moved to a different stall and water turned on about ten feet away. She sighed in relief and worked the soap into her hair even faster, still keeping a wary ear on the other shower occupant. Kira was grateful for the shower. If all runners had instant access to hot water like this, then if she survived, she may very well think about running again just to have a shower.

Living on the streets was hard, and she'd almost forgotten how good it felt to be clean. When she was done, she looked around for something to dry herself off with and found nothing. She was about to pull aside the curtain and look when something burst through.

THIRTEEN

Kira screamed as the shower curtain tried to smother her face. She gripped the knife in her hand and swung at the plastic sheet, stabbing, jabbing, and swinging. Her screaming brought others. The door burst open as Zeke and Chaz stormed into the room looking for an attacker. Kira struggled with the shower curtain she'd attacked and ripped down from the bar. It wasn't easy to get the clingy shower curtain off her but keep it between her body and the guys.

A girl specter floated feet away in a frenzied motion. Her translucent hands kept waving and pointing at the offending towel she had tried to pass through the curtain to Kira. The towel that Kira had thought was attacking her was now lying in a puddle on the floor.

Her cheeks burned with embarrassment—for so many reasons. She did her best to grip the shower curtain to cover up all important areas of her body.

Chaz started laughing. His throaty laugh had a weird hiccup to it, as if the werecheetah wasn't used to laughing. Zeke raised one eyebrow at her in disbelief. Even the occupant of the last stall timidly peeked out to see what the ruckus was—Amazon woman. When she saw Kira's towel on the floor, she shook her head and ducked back into her stall. After mocking and laughing at her till they were satisfied, both the male runners left the bathroom.

Kira grabbed her makeshift curtain-towel and the sopping wet one from the floor and dashed down the corridor into another dressing area. Quickly, she pulled on the provided uniform and fingered the white material. It wasn't pretty, didn't do that much to enhance her figure, and reminded her of burlap.

The seasoned, talented runners had darker expensive uniforms befitting their stations—the darker the uniform, the better the runner. The newbies wore usually white, Ferb had said. A blank canvas for the blood. It also screamed, *Hey! I'm right here. Kill me.*

She supposed it helped the spectators—they could focus on the red and black uniforms and place bets. And it must be nice and easy to watch the new runners get picked off like flies. The order of rank went white, gray, red, black.

Kira tied the laces of her boots and sat silently on the bench, contemplating her last moments. Soon, they would be marked and numbered. Statisticians would collect their data and snap a quick photo of the last minute entries. Then the cart would pick them up and deliver them to the course where they would meet with their sponsors for last minute encouragement. There would be the harvest of gifts, if any'd been given, and they would line up for the race, in the order of color.

She started shivering and began to flex her fingers and run her hands through her damp hair. Her specter floated a few feet from her, bobbing gently in the air, waiting to come if bidden. Kira gave the girl an ugly glare, before giving in and motioning her over to finish her job.

The iridescent specter smiled brightly and whisked behind her to run a comb through her hair. The light, ethereal fingers brushing against her scalp felt way more comforting than she'd expected. When was the last time someone had brushed her hair?

Her father. Just remembering him brought stinging tears to her eyes. She quickly wiped them away.

When the specter was done styling her hair, she handed Kira a mirror. Her hair was pulled away from her face into a high ponytail. Thin, little braids had been softly interwoven into her hair and down her ponytail. It gave her the appearance of being both soft and hard. Kira liked it.

A tall woman came in and addressed the runners, giving them the order of the events for the afternoon. All first time runners were to follow her out the door. Kira got in line behind a small bear-creature and was ushered into a large bunker.

There, a tall green man with horns poked, prodded, measured and photographed her, entering everything into a tablet. He put a tourniquet around her arm and pulled out a syringe.

"What are you doing?" Kira asked.

"Taking a blood sample."

"What for?" She winced when he pricked her skin and had to look away while the syringe slowly filled with her deep red blood.

"We run a test, check for impurities, see if anyone has had any genetic enhancements." He smiled, revealing pointed incisors.

"Really?"

The doctor snorted and shook his head. "No, not really. You're a new champion, so we take your stats and enter them into our computer. We also use your DNA to help identify the remains." He pulled out the needle and capped the vile of blood, wrote on it with a pen, and laid it down on the tray next to a lot of other filled samples. "If there are any left, that is."

Her eyes followed the vial and she read the label on her blood.

```
Race: Human
Name: Kira Lier
Owner: Remus Carthage
Blood Type: O+
```

Her stomach fought and tried to eject what little was inside, but she gritted her teeth and stared the doctor down.

"You won't need it." Totally feigning bravado, but he visibly squirmed under her dead eye scrutiny.

"Okay then, I need it for everyone else," he replied and looked away.

A loud scream erupted from across the room as one of the doctors flew across the room and slammed into a wall of cabinets. He slid onto the ground and didn't stir.

Kira scanned the direction of the growing crowd, and watched as nurses and doctors fled from one particular corner, where a large panicked beast fought the staff with the needles. He picked up his examining table and tossed it. Her heart stopped as the metal examining table flew in her direction. She dropped to the ground but the young doctor standing next to her didn't. Another victim.

Kira crawled along the ground seeking shelter from the manic monster attacking anyone in his wake. An alarm sounded and doors slammed, locking them inside. Kira could see the horned doctor motioning feebly towards her. She hesitated, debated leaving him, but a fragment of human compassion flickered. She scooted toward the doctor, keeping one eye on the possible threat from across the room.

It was bad, he wasn't going to survive. She could tell his lung was punctured, but he didn't seem to care. He just kept waving with his fingers towards the vials of blood scattered unbroken on the floor. Searching, searching for one in particular. Finally, he found what he was looking for and held it to his chest.

"You ducked." He laughed and started to choke.

"You didn't." She tried to smile back but couldn't.

"But you're human."

"Yeah, it's pretty obvious."

"You're fast. Take it." He handed her the vial.

"What is it?"

"Everlasting life," he smiled wanly, his eyes losing clarity. "Or at least healing."

"That's okay, this life sucks. Why would I want to live it forever?"

"Which is exactly why you should have it. It's unicorn blood."

"Nope, if it's that great, you take it. You're the one who needs it." She forced the tube back into his hand.

Instead, he shook his head and pushed back and closed her hands tight around the vial.

"No. You ducked." And then without further instructions or clues, he died.

Kira stared at the doctor, waiting to feel grief at his death, but since she didn't know him, there wasn't any. Grabbing the vial, she glanced at it briefly to see it was filled with a pearlescent ooze. She tilted it and it caught the light—it had a gold tint in it.

Screaming continued in the background, and soldiers busted into the room with black uniforms and helmets with long Tasers on rods. Someone reached a far wall and pulled a switch.

The room went black. A high pitched screech of pain rang out as the soldiers subdued the monster in question. Only the green glow from the soldier's night vision helmets alerted anyone to any movement. Every few moments, the electric blue light of the Taser sticks illuminated the nightmare.

She barely had the vial in her hand, when a searing jolt shot through her entire body. Paralyzing pain erupted, and her muscles spasmed as she crumpled to the floor. The vial rolled across the floor, crushed under the black boots of the soldier who'd shocked her.

The liquid pooled under his boot. Kira tried to reach for it but was cut off by more guards.

The Taser stick came into view, and the other side of the room erupted into flashing blue and white light as they continually Tasered the beast. A beast who was probably just as scared as Kira, trying to run away from the doctors and this nightmare. At the rate the soldiers were attacking, they were going to Taser it to death.

Another shock seared her body and she clenched her teeth in pain. She realized in that moment, she was more saddened at the unnamed beast's imminent death than the doctor's.

FOURTEEN

Someone was nudging her head—and they weren't letting up.

Kira looked out through half-lowered lids to see Chaz's feline eyes studying her with curiosity. He was too close for comfort, and his whiskers brushed her cheeks. This time he poked her in the in stomach. Her muscles were sore and felt lax, but she had enough control to fling an arm straight into his smug face.

He jumped back at the slap. "This one's not dead yet," he yelled. Kira could have sworn he seemed almost relieved.

Specters floated into the room. Those who weren't wounded were hauled into another room. Those who couldn't move were left for dead. Kira was surprised when Chaz picked her up and moved her to the main room. She found herself in a prime position on a couch.

"What happened?" she asked, looking around at the mellowed and somber faces of the group of competitors.

"You tell me. You were the one in there."

"I'm not sure. Someone was scared and threw a table, and then it got bad really fast."

"Half of the room didn't make it out, as you can see." He nodded as more and more specters floated out without a person accompanying them. The room filled with more competitors, and Chaz stepped back. He wore a black uniform. "And half more will never cross the finish line." His grim expression confused her as he looked at her and then away. "I don't think you'll get lucky twice."

She wanted to shout at him, but he disappeared into the throng of red and black-garbed competitors coming out of their rooms.

By now, everyone had heard what had happened. An added tension filled the air. She quickly got off the couch and moved to a wall where she could observe the group.

There must have been at least sixty—that she could see—inside the building. From the way the room numbers constantly changed, it seemed as if a lot more waited outside. Kira tried to stay away from the black and red groups and found herself sticking among the other white uniformed runners. It didn't help. The small pack of white runners found themselves the scrutiny of many hungry and dangerous beasts. She probably should have tried to make friends with the other first time racers, but she didn't. There was too much she wanted to see. It did seem that most of them were there because the lottery had chosen them.

Kira felt a moment's jealousy. Even the Amazonian woman had on a gray uniform. The color made her skin look sickly, but it at least proved she had survived a few events. Kira craned her head and tried to find Zeke among the white uniforms, but she couldn't see him.

They all watched the screen as bets came in. Kira had 50-1 odds of surviving. Her picture was dead last on the ranks. A heavy feeling of dread sank into her stomach. She could chose to let it bother her, could cry over it. Or she could go to that dark place, the place where she let her mind go when she didn't want to feel anymore. The place she'd retreated every time she was sick of hunger, or cold, or hurt. It was safe there.

Someone bumped Kira and she ignored it.

The noise in the waiting room died down, and she knew it was time to go. Staff directed them down a hallway and separated them by color into different elevators. Kira moved into her glass elevator and the large group of newbies came in with her. When the glass door closed, the small space filled with the scents of institutional soap and something else—fear.

She could *smell* their fear. She closed her eyes and tried to not look at the others. She couldn't—wouldn't—make eye contact. The eyes were the window to the soul. If she looked, it would knock her out of her small safe zone.

The doors to the second elevator opened, and she watched it fill with the gray champions. The third was filling with red, and then black competitors moved into their elevator. She turned to face the back of the elevator and looked out over the underground gorge. The building they were in was hundreds of feet up in the air, and the event starting line was down below them. All along the gorge, rows of seats carved out of stone were packed with thousands of fans gathered to watch the event.

"Look there," a large man said with distaste. "The Underlords."

Where he pointed, Kira saw a long coach pulled by black horses edging the top of the gorge. It kept going until it was out of sight. Did they have a separate viewing area? Probably. An owners' box or something. When she looked back down, her stomach dropped at the height.

She kept doubting herself, doubting everything, and yet there was a thrill of adrenaline that rushed through her. She clung to that feeling—she needed to ride that wave—so she focused on it.

Listening to the event organizer and the talk among the other champions, she'd learned that the elevator would drop, and the white gate would open. They'd all have to run like rabbits with greyhounds chasing them down. Shortly after, the gray car would drop and release the next group of champions, and so on and so on.

The whites' goal was to cross the finish line alive. The others groups' goals—stop the white runners from crossing. That was it. Simple enough, except that there were no rules regarding how they were to stop the white runners. They could delay them, capture them, tie them up—

Or kill them.

Kira saw Chaz's head towering over everyone in the black elevator and realized why he had chosen to compete. Who could outrun a shapeshifting cheetah? What if he was there to make sure she didn't cross the finish line?

Kira tasted blood. She'd bitten the inside of her cheek. She couldn't focus on him. She had to focus on the problem at hand. Outrunning the others in this car. If she could stay ahead of this group, she'd be less likely to get picked off.

The deeper they lowered, the closer they came to the gorge floor, the more the tension rose in the elevator car. People started jumping, flexing, shaking their legs, preparing to sprint as soon as the door opened. They surged toward the door they'd entered.

But the runners in the other cars were facing the gorge. Kira scanned the back wall and noticed a mechanism above—it would raise the glass wall and let them straight out onto the rocky track.

Loud horns blared throughout the gorge, slightly muffled by the near soundproof glass. The people in the gorge walls started to stand and cheer. A giant projector flashed the names of the runners in the first car, and Kira stared up at her own name on the cavern wall.

She'd always wanted to see her name in lights, but not like this.

The glass elevator touched down, and the runners began to push and pry the door open. Kira waited for the glass door to lift. The glass slid upward, but ground to a stop with an awful scraping sound. The back door had only opened eight inches.

"Open the doors!" Someone shouted and began to pound on the door frantically. A huge fist punched the glass, but it didn't break or shatter. It was reinforced.

"Maybe they'll reset the clock and let us start again?" a girl asked.

Kira bet the gray elevator's door wasn't going to stick. "I wouldn't count on it." She immediately dropped to her hands and knees and began to slide under the eight-inch gap. The tight squeeze required a lot of twisting. As soon as she slid through, the grinding noise came again. It closed to six inches—an impossible amount of room for any of the other runners to make it out.

The crowd erupted at her progress, and she turned and looked at the path in front of her. She should run. She'd have a huge advantage.

"Go! Run!" The girl inside yelled at Kira. She held up her arm against the glass and motioned for her to go. Kira saw her band. Red numbers. She was here because of the debt she owed.

Kira shook her head in disgust. "Come on, everyone!" Kira yelled, dropping to her knees. She lifted, prying, pulling against the machine with all her strength. The girl caught on and reached down to help.

Others quickly joined in. Inch by inch, they pulled the door up until it was two feet off the ground. But the grinding noise started again, and the timed door worked against them.

They were going to lose what little ground they'd gained.

The girl slid out first. Instead of helping, she looked fearfully up at the gray elevator, turned and ran. The runners slid out one by one. Inside, a large, pale man with a horn for a nose, and a smaller bird-like beast were helping Kira hold the door open for the others.

"Go!" The rhino-man commanded. His breath left a mist across the glass. The bird took his advice and slid under the door. The rhino yelled in pain as the door closed another foot. He wouldn't make it out.

"You too. Go."

"But you'll be left alone." Kira heard the gray elevator—only a hundred yards above her to her right.

"You could have just left us, but you didn't. I'll sacrifice myself for you." He placed his large hand against the glass, and Kira matched him against the other side. His massive palm dwarfed hers.

Then the beast turned, crossed his arms, and closed his eyes. Waiting for the inevitable. Kira heard the gray team pounding on the glass as they lowered the final few yards.

She was out of time. She spun to run.

But her steps faltered. Such dignity in his eyes. Such malice in her. How could she possibly deserve his sacrifice?

She wouldn't let it be in vain. Her legs pumped like pistons and she shot down the path like an arrow from a bow. The second elevator opened and the gray team was released. She looked over her shoulder and saw most of the runners had bypassed the beast imprisoned in the glass. Maybe he was too easy of a catch?

A blur of gray passed her, and she barely had time to register the thing running ahead of her. Whatever it was leapt into the air and brought down someone in white. She heard a quick cry. Kira didn't even look, just kept running, using her arms to propel her faster. She could see some of the other runners slowing ahead of her, and she was quickly overtaking them. They hadn't paced themselves and she wasn't either.

She needed to watch out for that. This wasn't a fifty-yard dash. The gauntlet was a marathon. Kira tried to slow her panicked breathing and find a rhythm she could keep. She couldn't burn out like the ones she'd just passed.

One

Two

Three runners left in her dust. Kira saw the image above her change, and she glanced up at the wall to see the projection of the last two elevators dropping. The camera zoomed in on the first white elevator. One of the red runners was attacking the elevator with the horned rhino man. A blur of black bolted out of the elevator. Kira knew Chaz was out and running for her.

She stumbled and grit her teeth. *Don't cry.* Just don't. It was impossible not to look up when they ran, and watch the red teams catch up and take out anyone they caught.

Kira breathed a moment of strange relief. White runners weren't the only target now. Everyone was.

A faun slowed in front of her as he stared in horror at the image displayed on the wall.

Kira almost plowed into him. "Run!" She maneuvered right to pass him and hit him on the shoulder. He stood absolutely frozen, distracted by what she assumed were gruesome images. Her heart thudded loudly, so she counted in her head to calm her nerves.

Her smooth path veered left and disappeared over a cliff. Whoa! She backpedaled, hands in the air. Her feet skidded as she almost tumbled over the hundred-foot drop. Down below she heard the pitiful cries and saw the odd angles of a few runners who hadn't managed to stop in time.

Kira studied the cliff. It could be scaled, but it would take time—time she didn't have. A red runner came up behind her, and Kira expected to be knocked over the edge, but he was only interested in racing. His arms morphed into giant eagle wings, and he flapped his arms a few strong times to gain a little altitude.

A crazy idea formed in her head.

She liked crazy.

She stepped back and gauged his distance. As he neared the edge, she paced him and leapt with him. At him, actually. She grabbed onto his uniform and joined him for the glide down.

"Let go!" He snapped his beak at her in frustration, his head and upper torso still in bird form. He couldn't use his arms to knock her off, or they'd both tumble from the sky. As they descended, he lifted his booted leg and tried to shake her off. She felt herself begin to slip, but glanced down. They'd nearly made the hundred-foot descent.

If she fell, she'd survive. For at least a moment.

"Thanks." Kira let go and tucked her body into a roll to ease her fall. Her landing was neither smooth nor elegant. Her back slammed into the hard rock, knocking her breath from her. Her chest and back ached. She saw stars. When she stopped rolling, she was lying face down on something soft, warm, and definitely unmoving.

***

Den had bitten his nails down to the quick as he paced the floor in the sponsors' box. He glanced back up at the TV screen and then back to the field below. Kira surprised him. With the way the betting started to turn in her favor, she was surprising a lot of people. Her odds had just gone up.

And the commentators keep replaying the elevator rescue over and over. As soon as the elevator gate didn't open, he looked over at Remus and knew. He had done something. He had paid, or manipulated someone, into jamming the gate in the hopes of killing the girl. Did he know Den had bet on her?

This time, if Den lost, he'd end up in the Gamblers' Market as a slave.

One smug look from Remus, and Den knew that had been his plan all along. Remus sat in his chair across the room. His ringed fingers lifted and he pointed to the pit where Kira'd just landed. Then he made a slicing motion across his throat.

Sweat trickled down Den's back. He looked back to see Bogeyman leap into the air to land on all fours in the pit, mere feet from Kira's prone form. He bit his thumb harder and tasted blood.

***

Kira, able to breathe and move again after a moment, turned her head. Her arm was stained bright red.

Don't look. She told herself. Keep going. She was about to push herself up when she heard something heavy land on the ground next to her. Instinct told her to stay very still.

Something huffed and scratched at the rock and bodies of the unfortunate runners who hadn't survive the jump. At that point, Kira couldn't have moved even if she wanted to. Fear had made her its slave. She closed her eyes and slowed her breathing.

The thing made its way over. Its claw moved across her body, and its horrid breath saturated the air around her as it leaned over her.

A faint cry of pain sounded in the distance and drew its attention away.

Kira opened her eyes and saw the heavily muscled back of the beast in a black uniform stalking toward the injured runner. Her gaze rose to see the shining white of a bald head. The bald thing rushed over toward the pained noises. Its large hand rose in the air and came down quickly.

The cries stopped suddenly.

The thing howled and moved further on its hunt.

More runners climbed down the wall, others jumped. The red and black teams had all run the course before—they knew about the cliff. A few had even teamed up to help each other.

The thing roared at them as they landed on the canyon floor. A few darted away as soon as they saw the beast.

Kira spotted a blur of black and yellow. Chaz was now ahead of her.

The other runners didn't scare her as much as the beast across from her. She couldn't stay. As soon as its back was turned, she jumped up and ran. She heard a loud howl, and the crowds cheered. She couldn't help but look up and see the camera zoom in on the thing's face—the stuff of nightmares.

A banner ran across the bottom of the image, its name and kill tally. That was the boggart—Bogeyman—and he had just finished off four at the bottom of the cliff. If she had stayed, she would have been just another kill, another number—five.

Up ahead, the course went into a darkened tunnel with no lights. The green light of another runner's bands bounced as they ran deeper into the tunnel. Those lights wouldn't turn off, she remembered unless someone was killed. Actually, they sort of created a beacon in the blackness. Not good.

A second later, the bobbing light disappeared, and she heard a scream. Her own light on her band would be the death of her in that dark tunnel.

Kira slowed and fell to her knees in front of a mud puddle. She craned her neck and watched as a red runner veered off course, coming her way. Quickly, Kira dove flat into the mud to make her white uniform dark. She scooped up a thick glob and covered the digital screen of her band, making the glowing light disappear. Stumbling to her feet, she ran head first into the darkened tunnel. She tried to cover the light with her hand too, but still—she expected the attack any moment.

FIFTEEN

Ten feet in it was pitch black.

Her eyes didn't adjust right away, so she ran as far as she could and then found a sidewall, feeling along the cold stone until she found an outcropping. Kira made herself as small as she could and pressed herself into it. She closed her eyes and counted.

She listened: to others running by her, to their cries as they found other runners, or as they stumbled about in the darkness.

It didn't take long for her human eyes to adjust. She was used to sorting out shapes in the darkness from living on the streets. She stayed to the side and tiptoed. Moving, freezing, then traveling farther into the blackness. She didn't know how long the tunnel went, but it dipped down so low that all natural light from outside was disappearing.

From where she stayed, she could see that the rocky tunnel was wide, about thirty feet across. A few runners had spread themselves across the middle and were intercepting others that tried to pass by them.

Chaz stood in the middle of them, his feline eyes probably easily seeing in the darkness.

Kira pressed herself to the wall—mud-covered side out—and tried to keep herself moving, using large rocks and stalagmites as cover. Sounds of a huge scuffle filled the air as she passed the middle of the tunnel. She winced but refused to look.

The stronger teams were now fighting against each other.

Kira made it past the midway point before Chaz noticed her. She was grateful that he was feline and sight-oriented, not driven by scent. When he did see her, he looked like he was about to come after her, but a blind runner practically plowed into him.

She took off, hugely grateful for the distraction and the time to put distance between Chaz and her. When she stumbled back into the light, she was surround by a forest of giant crystals that jutted at odd angles out of the ground and walls. Natural or unnatural, it was still a sight to behold. Oh, she wanted to touch it. Her hand moved on its own, closer to the crystals. Closer.

Someone came crashing off the path in front of her. He was screaming at her, and she turned to see a wild-eyed champion in gray. He plowed over her and she fell backwards, his body landing on top of hers. His pupils were dilated and practically spinning in hollowed sockets. He was foaming at the mouth. Ferb had warned her these were like the small ones in the cavern. The ones that made humans crazy.

If that was the case, then…was he some sort of a halfling?

How would *she* make it through?

She pushed him off and rolled to her knees, staring at the crystal in front of her. It was very pretty. So pretty.

She dragged her eyes away from it, and they ached from the effort. But she couldn't stay where she was. She had to keep moving.

Gritting her teeth, Kira continued into the crystal forest. She'd have to keep her eyes on the ground. The path wasn't straight. After a few times in its circular grip, she could tell what it did—she just couldn't beat it. It would veer right, split off into a fork, and she must've kept taking the wrong path, because she'd be back at the mouth of the tunnel.

She hid a few times when others ran past. Watched them.

Trumpets blared. How long had she been in this place? She glanced up and saw the projected image on the wall in front of her instead of crystals. It was showing the first runner crossing the finish line. A runner in gray.

Followed by a second runner in gray.

The screen flashed back to the course, zooming in on the crystal section she was currently on. She saw herself and noticed that she had almost made it through. Once she got out, it would be a straight run for the finish line.

A renewed burst of determination fueled her. She kept her eyes focused downward and continued to try and run, but she began to feel sick—a pull on her mind. Why was it so hard to focus?

Diamonds littered the ground in front of her. She faltered, slowed, could feel herself start to give up. The crystals were so, so mesmerizing. So comforting, and she wanted to have them all. She reached down to pick one up, just as a body rammed into her and they went rolling along the ground.

Bogeyman. The man-beast snapped at her, baring his teeth in a fierce growl. When it came for her jugular, she shoved her band into its mouth and punched at its bald head.

Her left hand found a broken piece of crystal. She aimed for its eye. Missed. She jabbed it in the side of the face.

The boggart reared back and shook its head.

Kira stared down the nightmare from her back position and tried to scoot away from it, but the ground began to give way behind her. Kira had reached the edge of a drop-off.

The boggart's pink-rimmed eyes were filled with fury. It snarled, revealing a row of uneven teeth covered with a dark wet substance she didn't care to dwell on. It howled and charged.

Kira gripped a long spear-like crystal and pulled it across her body. Waited.

The boggart lunged, and Kira lifted the spear, aiming for the stomach. She heard it cry out in pain, but it continued to scratch at her forearms and face. Adrenaline flooded her, and she used her feet to launch the boggart over her head and over the edge. Its mouth opened in shock as it fell over the side.

She listened to its fading howl.

***

"Nooo!" Remus rose from his chair screaming in outrage. His own cry echoed that of his boggart. "That can't be!" He couldn't believe that the human girl killed his boggart. He spun around to give Den a piece of his mind, but his trainer had vanished. The door was slowly swinging close at his hasty departure.

Well, that was smart. It probably saved his life. Now Remus hoped that someone—maybe Den's zeke—would finish killing the girl. If it miraculously crossed the line, he'd make sure it would have an accident.

An annoying high pitch staccato laugh erupted from the only other occupied chair. Peter, the rabbit, spun his chair around easily and taunted Remus, "And to think, I almost bought that one."

***

Kira pulled herself up and struggled down the path toward the finish line. Her feet were dragging, her arm hanging loosely at her side. The diamonds were everywhere, and she tried to close her eyes, but her brain wouldn't obey. She just wanted one—no. No. She had to stop it. She fell to her knees and used the edge of a broken diamond to tear off part of her uniform. With everything she had left, she focused on the finish line, then tied the scrap of material around her eyes.

It took a few precious seconds before the insane desire to rip it off faded. Kira pushed herself to her knees and jogged forward.

Blindly, she choked down her fear, and ran. Her brain tried to guess how, exactly, she would die.

Focus.

She ignored the sound of running footsteps catching up to her. Forward. Someone pushed her down, and she tumbled to the ground. Her palms took the brunt of the fall and the cuts from the diamonds.

Now she was turned around, unsure where to go. Trembling, she walked her hands out in front of her like a blind person, feeling, in case she got turned around and was about to run into a jagged crystal or go over the cliff.

But even without seeing the crystals for more than a few seconds, the madness began to worm its way into her mind. It was worse than she had feared. She wanted that blindfold off. Her hand itched to reach for it. Both hands tingled, and she raised one to take off the blindfold. Give up.

A warm hand grabbed hers and pulled. Kira started to scream, but a familiar and impatient voice cut her off. "This way."

Zeke.

She lifted the blindfold and saw his crazed hunger-filled eyes. She tried to pull her hand from his grip.

"No, keep going. You have to cross. Can't you hear it?" he asked.

Hear what? The only thing she heard now was the pounding of her own blood in her ears.

"I can't." Her mouth felt like it was swollen. She was losing control of her limbs.

"Here." He pulled something out of a pouch that looked very familiar. Wait, she had given him that pouch. He shoved a piece of chocolate into her mouth. It melted across her tongue, and she almost moaned in pleasure. Her mind started to clear, and even though her legs still weren't working, she was able to direct herself.

"Run, I'll guide you. If anyone tries to stop you, I'll take care of them." He gently pushed her blindfold back down over her eyes and turned her toward the finish line. "That way."

He pushed her roughly from behind, and she was jarred back into a run. She couldn't help but feel like Creeper was chasing her again.

A strange rhythm kept her moving forward.

A hiss came from her right, and a loud scuffle followed.

Zeke's voice sounded farther off. "Keep going!" he yelled.

Then Kira heard it. Heard what he had been hearing when all she could make out was the call of madness. Now she heard the *crowd.* Heard the thrum of their voices, mingling as one. She'd only thought it was a drum. It was actually her name.

They were chanting her name.

Kira Lier…Kira Lier.

She couldn't help the smile that crept up on her face. It was painful, her lip swollen. The chanting became louder, faster, and she knew she was almost to the finish line.

Over and over she heard her name. A thundering rush of applause—for her. She knew she had crossed. She heard her name over the speakers, and she slowed. Took off the blindfold.

She blinked painfully. The lights burned her eyes. She turned and looked behind her just as Zeke took out a reptilian monster. His hands were deft and quick. The kill fast. He jogged a few more paces and crossed the finish line as well, but he wasn't received with the same applause.

His eyes narrowed and he bowed his head in her direction, acknowledging her victory. He looked up and pointed. Kira craned her neck and was puzzled by what she saw.

Someone stood there in a dirt-covered, blood-covered uniform. Their eyes looked a little feral—the person seemed on edge.

She froze. It was her.

Kira Lier appeared on a banner, and next to her name a ranking and her kill stat. She was surprised to see a slash mark at all by her name.

But it was there. One horrible slash mark.

Her name chanted over and over began to blur in her ears. She didn't hear Kira Lier coming from the fans around her. In her head, as guilt wrecked her mind, the chant slowly morphed.

Kira Lier

Kiralier

Killer.

Killer.

SIXTEEN

Kira bent over, her hands on her knees as her stomach rolled in protest at what she had done. Zeke handed her a bucket, and she moved to the side of the course as bile erupted.

"Congrats!" he said wryly between her dry heaves. "You survived."

"Shut it," Kira snapped back. She pushed stray strands of hair out of her eyes and slowly stood up. She brought up her arm to wipe her mouth but then looked at the stuff covering it and almost puked again.

A towel appeared in her hand, and Kira looked over at a young girl with eyes the size of tea saucers. She wore the clothes and hairstyle of a slave.

"Thanks," Kira said as she wiped at her mouth.

"You spoke to me," her breathy voice answered. Her giant eyes opening wider, she squealed in excitement and fled.

"And you created a fan base with your crazy antics."

"What antics?" Kira stared at Zeke.

"Oh, risking your neck to help open the elevator tube. It was smart to help them—created more targets. If you were the only one who was ahead of the gray team, you would have been easy pickings."

"That's a horrible thing to say. That wasn't the reason I helped them."

He shrugged his shoulders. "You were pretty ruthless, jumping on Talon and making him fly you to the bottom of the gorge. Then you showed smarts when you covered your band and hid in the tunnels."

"How do you know all of this?"

"I watched you do it."

"You could have taken me out."

"Yes, I could have. But you intrigue me. I wanted to see how far you'd get on your own, and then I had to repay you for the chocolate." He patted the bag tied to his waist.

This was the first time she had taken a close look at him. He was dressed head to toe in a red uniform. No wonder she couldn't find him among the new runners. But he looked so young. How long had he been competing? How many kills were under his belt?

Kira looked up at the screen and tried to find his name among the list of ranked competitors and then she realized—she had been calling him Zeke in her mind for so long. She didn't even know his name.

She was desperate to ask him more questions, but they were ushered off the track to make room for the rest of the groups coming across. They were taken up to a viewing ledge with refreshments and chairs as they watched the last competitors complete the course. Way fewer runners finished than what started the race.

Very few white runners survived.

The next couple of hours were a daze. She was interviewed and then pawed at as people touched her for luck when she passed among the fans. She grimaced and pulled back at first, but then she saw that it was all part of the lifestyle. Zeke took each of the pats with grace and stopped to shake the outstretched hands. It seemed this came with the territory of being a champion. He was either used to it, or he was able to put on a good show.

Kira kept her chin up and tried to not cringe from the onslaught of affection. Especially when that affection was accompanied by growls and large clawed hands that could easily maim and kill her.

The remaining runners rode in a separate glass elevator and were taken to another room. Camera flashes blinded her. When the spots cleared, she saw a very large dais. Remus stood among the other owners.

"What do you think about today's outcome?" A merwoman with white hair asked the gym owners and trainers.

"I think the outcome was quite obvious, Avis," a stoic trainer said. His tan cheeks were sunken in, giving him weathered, aged look. "My fighters would have performed better but I—and I'm not alone in this—I believe it was because of a malfunction with the starting gate." His eyes flashed, showing the first hint of emotion. "There should have been a delay. They should have started over."

"You would have lost all of your starters if it wasn't for the one from Remus's gym," the female vamp interjected. Kira recognized her from the Gamblers' Market. "I was the one who lost Rhinoc to the gate malfunction."

Even some of the owners appreciated her. Kira let the thought encourage her.

"That's a human for you!" Ssirone called out. "Too stupid for its own good. Letting their emotions take control."

Well…

"Who dares to insult the human fighter?" The vampire's powerful voice rang out across the room. She must have recently fed, because the apple of her cheeks flushed a rosy color.

"Why would you care about humanssss when they're nothing more than food to you?" Ssirone yelled at Selene.

"Remus," Avis directed her next question to the man. His arms were crossed and his brows furrowed. His posture alone spoke of his displeasure at being interviewed. "Were you surprised when your human was drafted? Weren't you afraid it would get eaten?"

Remus looked up. The furrowed brow smoothed, and his face took on an almost pleasant demeanor. "I'm surprised that she lived, but I won't underestimate her so easily again." His gaze flicked over to Zeke and Kira. A chill gripped her spine. He looked back to the reporter. "Every event is a gamble. And I like to gamble big."

"And win," Avis smiled sweetly. "I do have to say that your human surprised us all and garnered herself quite a lot of adoration when she killed the boggart. She's quite the fighter isn't she?"

"Yes…she…is," Remus locked eyes with Kira, and then he flicked over to where Den was standing.

Kira studied the pompous owner. On the outside he was cool, nonchalant, but Kira knew he was anything but—he was likely plotting her demise. First she'd killed Creeper, and now his new boggart as well. He'd already wanted her dead. What would he do now to make sure it happened?

Zeke seemed to have picked up on the exchange and stepped in front of Kira, drawing Remus's attention toward himself, which only made Remus's face go redder. *He might lose his cool here in front of everyone.*

"Ironically, your human took out your own boggart. I also heard a rumor that she killed one of your zekes the first day at the training gym. Am I correct?" Avis turned, directing her question toward Remus. "Would you like to comment on this?"

Remus snarled in displeasure but quickly forced it into a smile. "Yes, I'm quite surprised by her ingenuity and skills. I doubt we will ever see the likes again." He stood and left the stage, ending the interview but leaving a hidden threat in the air.

The chatter around her picked up with excitement, while Kira's heart plummeted in fear. She looked up at Zeke and noticed that his cheeks looked sunken and his eyes were rimmed in red. He swallowed and gave her a wary look.

"Come, it's time to see our medic."

Seventeen

From Remus's compound, only Zeke, Kira, and Chaz made it back to their assigned room. There was very little to celebrate. Kira tried as hard as she could to remember passing the Amazon woman or the other man, or even seeing them in the race. She couldn't. How far had they made it?

Now that the race was over, it was up to the owner's doctor to treat the survivors. Kira couldn't help but stare around the room that hours earlier had been torn apart. The cabinets and tables—a few of them dented—had been righted, the broken chairs were piled haphazardly in a corner. Kira tried not to look at the darkened stain on the floor where her pre-game doctor had died.

Now they each sat on a chair while Warrick examined and bandaged each of them. There was very little privacy.

Chaz had a large wound on his shoulder—like something or someone had tried to take a bite out of him. Warrick applied a topical cream, but whenever he wasn't looking, Chaz would bend his agile neck and lick the wound frantically.

Warrick came back and examined the wound. "Stop licking it off. You'll infect it," he warned, giving Chaz a scathing look. Kira tried not to laugh at him, even though he reminded her of her own childhood cat.

Chaz just purred, a soft rumbling noise coming from his part-feline vocal chords. His eyes closed and he looked to be content.

Warrick raised an eyebrow before applying more ointment. "Hmm. I guess I'll just have to bandage it then to keep you from bothering it." He went to the cabinet. Again, as soon as his back was turned, Chaz's furious licking continued. Warrick turned suddenly from the cabinet with a spray bottle and squirted a surprised Chaz in the face.

Chaz hissed once—the first moment he seemed more cheetah than housecat—and then sat quietly as Warrick wrapped a bandage around his shoulder and under his arm. Chaz was obviously uncomfortable. The muscles on his chest kept twitching. And it looked like he really wanted to tear it off.

"Sit there," Warrick commanded Chaz. He turned to examine her.

Using scissors, he cut away at the sleeves of her uniform to get to the gash on her arm. Kira had been so pumped with adrenaline that she hadn't even noticed the injury. She had no idea when or how she'd sustained it. Of course, now that it was visible, it was extremely painful. And her shoulder burned, too.

"So you survived the gauntlet," Warrick stated, matter of fact.

"Ye-s-s," Kira sucked in air with a painful hiss. She could feel the gazes of Chaz and the zeke, so she cut off the sound. She wouldn't give them the satisfaction of knowing how much pain she was in. She could hide it. She had to.

There was a long pause.

"Good."

A heaviness hung in the air. She could tell he wanted to say more, but it was safer to stay silent among the present company. He used a flask or two on her wounds, and then bandaged her shoulder and a few more cuts along her face and leg.

Zeke was barely moving, sitting quietly on the end of the table, his head hung low.

"Let me see." Warrick unzipped his red uniform, and Kira saw a blotch of red across Zeke's white t-shirt. The red uniform hid his bleeding completely. He pulled down the top half, and Kira saw a small pipe sticking out of his side.

"Oh, this is not so great," Warrick mumbled under his breath. "Why didn't you say anything?"

Zeke raised his head slowly, and he looked over at Kira. His sunken eyes seemed even hollower, his eyes dilated. There was a wildness about him, like he was lost in a hunger and he didn't have control of all of his faculties.

"Oh, I see." He looked over at Kira and motioned to Chaz. "Take her out of the room, please. I need to remove the pipe, and she is too much of a distraction. It will be safer for both of us if she's gone."

Chaz slid off the end of the table with feline grace and headed out the door. He didn't even wait for her. She wasn't sure if following him out was the safest thing to do, but Zeke's breathing started to hitch, and Warrick's voice rose in panic.

"Go, Kira! Now!"

She jumped off the table and flung herself out the door. A few seconds later, she heard footsteps pounding after her and the door slammed behind her. Something large crashed into the door, followed by a frenzied scuffle from behind the metal door. She heard Warrick's calming voice.

Kira backed away in fear and bumped into Chaz.

"You almost bit it," Chaz wheezed. His unhindered arm slapped his thigh. "You should have seen the look on your face."

She heard a snarl and another slam against the metal door. "Is he going to be okay?" Kira asked, not sure if she was referring to Zeke or Warrick.

"Yeah, Warrick's got him under control."

"How do you know?" Her voice sounded so young.

Chaz pointed at his ears. "'Cause I can hear them. Warrick's calming him down. He's praying right now."

"Praying?"

"Some call it mojo, others magic. If you ask Warrick, he says he's praying in an ancient language to quicken Zeke. That was a pretty serious injury he got there. He'll have to knock him out or let him feed…and if that's the case. There's one especially tasty treat right here." Chaz leaned closer, his deep amber eyes lit up with mischief. His mouth came dangerously close to her face. He licked his lips and took a deep breath, his face almost touching hers as he moved it along her cheek. "Yumm." She could hear a deep thrum in his throat.

Kira pushed him away in disgust.

"Relax, I'm not interested in eating you whole, but I may be satisfied with a bite." He pulled back and bit his lower lip, his canines visible. Kira cringed.

The door opened and Warrick stepped out.

"How is he?" Kira asked.

"He'll be fine. But it would be best if you are nowhere near him while he's healing."

"I don't understand."

"It's a zeke thing. When they're injured, they can go a bit berserk. Their brain shuts down while their body is trying to heal. Eating… ahem… helps them heal faster." He didn't say it but Kira knew what he implied.

Her.

"It would be best if he doesn't see you for a while. This was a bad one. He shouldn't revert this fast. His history as a fighter is finally catching up to him. It'll do that, you know. Some of us have been fighting a long, long time."

Kira was about to ask him more questions, but Warrick told them it was time to collect. She had no idea what collecting meant.

EIGHTEEN

It was time to pay. As they lined up to leave Crystal Gorge and head back to Remus's compound, they had to pass through a large machine that resembled an airport security device. Chaz had pressed through the lines and cut in front of quite a few monsters to stand precariously close to Kira's back.

Kira, only a few bodies from entering, was wary of the whole process. With Chaz's breath hot on her neck, she tried to keep an eye on what was happening to the creatures in front of her.

She elbowed Chaz roughly, and he backed off a bit. But then something caught his attention. He sniffed the air, and his feline eyes narrowed on the lizard in front of him. "Watch closely," Chaz whispered under his breath. "You are about to get a show."

"What do you mean?" Kira turned her head slightly so she could hear him, but still watch the line in front. The monster that was currently in the airport looking scanner passed through, and another one took its spot.

"I smell a shifter," he whispered.

"You mean yourself?"

He chuckled. "No, I'm a lycanthrope—a werecat. I can only shift into my cheetah form or any stage in between. Shifter is different. They can morph into anything they've seen, and they have a unique scent when they shift."

"You can tell just by smell?"

"Everything smells down here, and pretty soon it's easy to pick out what doesn't belong. But I think we have a cheater." He nodded toward a runner with scales stepping up to the large machine. A short dwarf woman manned a computer console and screen behind a glass wall. She was the one overseeing the dispensing of tokens.

"Name?" Her voice came out with a static undertone.

"Targrit," the guttural name came out of the tall, scaled monster. The dwarf looked over at him, her eyes cold and calculating.

Chaz was behind her, and he seemed agitated. "Don't do it, man. It's not worth it," he breathed out. Only Kira was close enough to hear it.

"Owner?" the woman asked, her hand slowly moving to a large red button.

"Free. I was drafted." The monster's lizard-like skin began to show a sheen of sweat across his brow. Reptilian monsters shouldn't sweat. What was going on?

The woman smiled slowly, her green teeth gnashing together in pleasure. "Enter."

"What's happening?" Fear raced up Kira's spine at the dwarf woman's pleasure.

"It's payout time. They match up your brace with your body to make sure they are loading your freedom tokens to the right person. From time to time, a shifter will steal a band off of a dead runner and try to claim the winnings. A heartbeat can fool the band, but only the strongest shifters are capable of fooling the machine." Chaz shifted his weight nervously.

"And that's what you think is happening here?"

"Watch and see," he answered.

As soon as the monster stepped up and into the machine, his body was scanned, and another face popped up on the screen. The shifter's real identity, which was a pale white being with spots, quite different than the reptilian he was portraying.

The dwarf woman hit the red button, and he shrieked—immediately trapped. Glass doors shut him inside the machine. "We have a cheater." She spoke into an intercom, and a crowd gathered around and started to boo and hiss loudly at the fake competitor. She pushed another few buttons on her console, and the floor dropped out from under him. He fell into a dark hole. Kira had no idea where it led to, but she had a feeling she never wanted to be suspected of cheating.

"Next!" The short woman perched on the tall stool yelled a little too happily.

Kira stood frozen, staring as the hole in the floor closed up with a whoosh of air. She was not going to step on that platform. No way.

"Next!" The control woman ordered, and Kira felt a nudge from behind her. She was next.

"Name?" The short woman on the tall stool watched her. Kira's eyes were glued to the floor, and the control woman had to ask twice more before Kira could tear her eyes away and answer her.

"Kira Lier."

"Owner?"

Owner. No one owned her. Her anger spiked. She refused to say anything. The line of other runners behind her was beginning to talk.

"Owner?" The short woman repeated a bit more impatiently.

"I am." Remus stepped up from the other side of the machine. He held up his bracer and put it against the metal reader on the exit side of the machine. Numbers flashed across the screen, and then there was a picture of her.

"Okay, step through."

Kira held her breath. All she could think was that the floor could open up and swallow her.

She stepped through and got scanned. Her stats came up on a viewing screen.

"Put your band against the plate."

She did. The plate beeped, and freedom tokens were loaded onto it—quite a few. Because she had killed the number one contender, Bogeyman, she got his winnings. Even more were loaded onto Remus's because he was her owner, and then it kept loading long after hers was done. His eyebrows shot upward when he read the amount.

Den stepped forward and placed his bracer against the plate.

He had placed bets. Who had he bet on?

"Underdog paid out big today." The short woman smiled wryly at Kira, showing her green and rotted teeth.

He bet on her.

She didn't understand the numeric system, but she understood money. Money meant freedom. As long as she could earn enough, she could leave. Her spirits soared.

Den gave her a pat on the head when she came out and didn't even look at his winnings. Remus stood behind Den, waiting to collect for Chaz. He was bouncing nervously—and wearing more jewels and decorations than she had seen him decked out in before.

Kira brought up her band to look at her winnings.

Remus gripped her wrist and twisted her arm, turning the brace so he could read the number.

It was odd. Kira felt violated, wanted to hold her hand over the screen and hide the numbers from Remus. She could almost see his mind plotting to steal her winnings. But then the whole exchange made her feel dirty. She did all of the work and Remus received money too—just for owning her.

"Maybe we got off on the wrong foot, the girl and I. Even though it's killed two of my prize runners now."

Chaz had just come through the machine, and Remus rubbed his hands together before moving to collect more winnings. "Yes, yes that's good." The number on his brace rose and kept rising. "You're doing well, Chaz. Won't be long now." Remus raised an eyebrow at him.

Chaz scowled and strode off into the crowd.

"Den." Remus turned and scanned the line. "Where's your zeke?"

"Infirmary," Den answered. "Warrick's taking care of him. He got injured protecting your runner, and now it's gonna cost me more money to fix him up."

"Maybe he should have minded his own business," Remus held out his arms, making his ornate robes flow beneath them. "I'd have made even more money on its death."

"He'll be fine." Den answered. But a sheen of perspiration peppered his forehead. He was nervous about something.

She backed away and bumped into Chaz who put his hands on her shoulders.

"I need winners, Den, not losers. Creeper and Bogeyman are busts. Chaz is a winner, certainly, but who knows how much longer he'll be with us. This is your problem twice over. Get me more winners."

"Maybe I'll help you out, and buy you out of your problem, Remus." He glanced over to Kira, and she felt a surge of hope. Maybe he could buy her.

Remus licked his lips and stared at Den's band. "Anything can be bought for the right price." His eyes flicked to Kira. "But sometimes I prefer death to money."

NINETEEN

A heaviness hung in the air as they left. Den and Warrick spoke in hushed voices, their conversation just quiet enough Kira couldn't make it out.

Zeke seemed to be improving—he got into the truck with little help. He did stay far away from her, though, leaning his head against the wall. And he wouldn't look at her. Did he feel bad for wanting to attack her in the medic room?

She kept glancing his way, trying to figure him out.

When they got back to the compound, an excited crowd greeted them. Holly was there—her black and purple eye had faded to a greenish yellow. Her mouth curled down with displeasure. Chaz jumped off the truck, and the first thing she did was hit him in the arm. A heated argument ensued, her hands flying and her voice rising.

Chaz glanced at Kira more than once and shrugged. She knew they were arguing about her. Was Holly upset that she came back alive? Probably.

She climbed down out of the truck and did her best to smile at those who smiled at her. Of course, with all the tusks and fangs in the group, she might've been mistaking a grimace for a smile.

Den came up behind her and pressed her back, urging her through the group. She hadn't realized she was scared of walking through the group until Den's nearness relieved her. No one would attack her with him watching over her. "Keep moving. I don't think it's safe for you to stay here much longer."

"Why?" she whispered between clenched teeth.

"Because you've now killed two of Remus's fighters. Money won't keep us safe for long. Take care, and stay close to the zeke. I've got business to finish up." Den gave her a pat on the shoulder, and she followed the other two closely through the crowd.

They made it back to the commons room, and Kira headed toward the table laden with hot food. A pang of hunger overcame her at the scent. Strange though, only three chairs sat around this glorious banquet. She felt uncomfortable standing around staring at it.

Chaz came in and pulled up a chair. "Eat." He gestured to the hot food.

"Why is no one else eating?" She pulled out a chair to stare at the mouthwatering food in front of her. It was obvious that someone had her in mind, because she could actually recognize some of the food. There was a pie—it looked and smelled like blueberry; fresh baked pizza covered in vegetables; and spaghetti marinara. Someone had been paying attention to what she had been eating, knew that she wouldn't touch anything with meat, knew that she missed human food. Kira picked up a slice the pizza off the plate and took a bite.

"The winners eat first. Whatever's left goes to the losers." Chaz stuck his finger in the middle of a pan of gravy-looking sauce and gave it a tentative lick. "Yum. It's a perk of winning."

Zeke sauntered in quietly and took a chair at the head of the table. He looked so regal sitting there as he reached over and took a turkey leg and placed it on a plate in front of him, as well as a dinner roll and some sort of tumor-looking vegetable. What surprised her, though, was that Zeke picked up a knife and fork and started to cut the meat off of the bone and slice his vegetables into bite size portions.

Kira had eaten a whole slice of pizza within seconds, and it had never touched her plate. She hastily brushed the crumbs off her fingers and eyed the rolled silverware next to her plate. She placed the napkin on her lap. Silverware gave her trouble, though. Mostly because she felt as if eyes were watching her, judging her.

She sliced into the blueberry pie and served herself a large portion. Taking a bite, she closed her eyes and savored the sweet taste. She finished off the rest within a few bites and looked over to Zeke. His lip rose a fraction of an inch in a smile, and then he dabbed at his cheek with his napkin.

He repeated the action.

Her eyes widened when she finally caught his drift. She took her own napkin and hastily wiped away a smudge of sauce on her cheek. How was it that he had better manners than she did?

Kira stared down at her plate as her cheeks warmed. Her appetite left her. She had been proven wrong on so many occasions over the last few days. Nothing was how she thought it would be. She came here expecting to hate everything and everybody, but she related to them. They were so much like her. Guilt gnawed at her gut.

Chaz leaned forward and swiped a finger in her pie filling. It froze inches from his mouth, and his nose twitched as he sniffed it warily. He sniffed it again and hissed, backing away.

"Nightshade," he growled. "Someone has tried to poison us."

Kira looked down at the crumbs—the only remains of the slice of pie she had just scarfed down. She held her hand over her mouth.

Zeke stopped eating and stood up. "Are you sure?" he asked Chaz.

Chaz studied the rest of the food on the table. "Hm. It wasn't in mine. I thought maybe I was getting too close to freedom." He moved over and sniffed, wrinkling his nose in distaste over the food next to Zeke, then came back around to the pizza and bread. "Nightshade mixed in with the veggies and bread. So, someone didn't want to poison *us*, just"—he pointed to the food that was spread out in front of her, catered to her human taste buds—"you."

The stomach ache she'd believed was guilt was now so much more painful as the reality hit her hard. She stood and stumbled.

Chaz knocked over the whole table of food in anger. He screamed and it turned into a high-pitched howl as if he already mourned her death.

Zeke appeared by her side. In a second flat, he had her arm wrapped around his head and scooped up her legs. He took off running toward the infirmary.

"Warrick!" He pounded on the door but no one answered. "Warrick!"

He carefully set her down by the door. "Kira, I have to find Warrick." You'll be okay. I'll be back. I promise." She felt his cool hand touch her burning cheek, and then he was off, his feet pounding on the cement floor. She pressed her forehead to the cold metal of the door and waited. A few seconds later, a door opened nearby. She clutched her stomach and whispered. "Help."

The steps moved away, thudding softly down the hall, never even pausing to help. Kira's vision swirled, but she tried to hold it together. She needed to find help before the poison could work its way through her system and end her suffering. She started to shiver and tried her voice again. "Help!"

"There you are!" A familiar voice called out, and Holly stepped out of the darkness, hands on her hips. "Did you get Remus's gift? I spent all morning baking it. Potions, spells, and poisons are my specialty."

A sharp stabbing pain pierced through Kira's side. She sucked in air through her teeth and tried to hold back the cries she desperately wanted to release. Biting her lip, she pulled herself up the door. She had to lean against the wall to walk, but she did it. Away from Holly—which direction didn't matter.

"Where you going?" Holly teased. Someone else stepped out of the darkness. A muscled Cyclops cracked his knuckles and grinned, showing his overlarge flat teeth. "I didn't say you could leave yet."

Kira took off. She wasn't in a fighting position. She could barely walk, cramps making her gait unsteady. Sweat ran down her face, and she couldn't stop shivering. But they didn't seem to be chasing her.

She heard Holly call out.

After a few blind turns, Kira made it to a door that seemed to lead out. She stumbled, fumbled, carelessly made her way down a path that she'd been down days earlier—toward the car graveyard.

Where was everyone?

Kira moved along, trying to not look towards the wreckage of the bus. She slipped and fell into a car, bruising her hip. She grunted and pushed herself up, trying to ignore the pain. A nearby car had an open trunk—an old Buick. The trunk was plenty large.

She painstakingly took her outer shirt off and crawled into the trunk. The carpet was rough and worn, like sandpaper under her palms. But it hardly mattered. She wasn't picking the car based on the interior carpet. She picked it because she hoped Holly and her goon wouldn't look for her here. If they passed by, she could slip out and head back toward help.

Kira's hands shook from the fever, and she had problems getting her muscles to do the simplest task without twitching. But after a few tries, she reached the lid of the trunk. This was it. There was no going back now.

Taking a deep breath to steady her nerves, she pulled the trunk down until only a sliver of light came through. Immediately, in the darkness, with nothing else to distract her, she could feel her body shutting down, feel the pain in her joints and the fever that raged against her. More stabbing pains came from her midsection, and she could no longer hold in a scream of pain that took everything from her. Wadding up her outer shirt she placed it into her mouth to muffle her whimpers.

A creaking noise came from above. Holly. "Where'd your fight go? Guess you're not much of a champion. Oh well, I guess that's what happens when you're out of your league." She smiled cruelly and reached in to grab Kira's arm band. With a few keystrokes and a touch of her own band—and then a transfer to the goon next to her—Holly wiped out her winnings. She dropped Kira's limp wrist like it was garbage.

Kira turned weakly and saw a bunch of zeroes across her wrist screen. All of her freedom tokens, gone.

"Thanks for sharing the wealth." Holly waved cheekily, and the trunk came down with a loud thud. Kira heard the lock click.

She was too weak to pound on the lid, and no one who cared was nearby anyway. Kira was going to die.

Normally, this would have bothered Kira, but when she considered her options, she was out of choices. Besides, it seemed reasonable. She was slotted to die anyway, Den had said it. Warrick confirmed her fears, and Remus was just finishing what Madame Fortuna had warned would happen.

Pain seized her suddenly, consumed her, and she cried into the gag, which she now spit out. Her body spasmed, and her foot launched out and kicked the trunk.

Kira would have thought her last moments of life would be spent replaying her happy childhood memories, but no. Her life unfolded before her in monstrous mini-episodes—stabbing her stepfather, running away from her mother, stealing food and wallets from unsuspecting vendors and marks. She revisited every memory she'd ever regretted.

The images played across the darkness of her mind like a horrific kaleidoscope. Then they turned darker: images of Creeper leading a mob of monsters on the hunt for her. She heard a whimper. Was that her? The trunk was so, so cold. She'd been suffering in the darkness for hours. Why hadn't she died yet?

Her head pounded with such intensity, she moaned. Maybe she would see her father soon. The pounding would stop and she'd see his face again.

Wait. No. That pounding was really happening—outside the car. Someone was outside the trunk of the car. They must have seen her get locked inside and were trying to get her out.

"Please, no," she cried out. "Go away so I can see my dad." But her voice was so faint and weak, she doubted they heard.

The pounding became more insistent.

The trunk bent, and a crack of light pierced the darkness. A worried voice told her she would be okay, and the pounding continued again. The light filled up more of the trunk. Kira squinted against the pain.

"No!" Her lungs burned and she coughed into her hand. When she pulled it away it was covered with blood.

"I'm coming!" Someone shouted and reached their hand through and tried to touch her arm. Kira rolled away from the touch; she found it hard to breathe and had to concentrate on every burning breath.

Just when the latch on the Buick broke, and the trunk was filled with unnatural fluorescent light, Kira stopped breathing.

TWENTY

She hadn't moved in a while. Zeke stared at Kira's limp body in the hospital bed and watched her closely, waiting for her to twitch, move—do something other than lie there helpless. She hadn't regained consciousness since he found her in the trunk and Warrick gave her the antidote.

Her eyes fluttered. He sighed in relief and leaned back in the wooden chair.

This was a problem. She was a problem. His feelings even more of a problem.

Den entered, trying to not make any noise, but failing. Zeke's senses were just too good. Den's breathing sounded loud in his ears, and he could hear his quickened heartbeat. Something was wrong. Den was worried about something.

Without moving he asked, "What's wrong?"

Den came out of the shadows. He stood by his shoulder and spoke in a low voice. "Everything."

"Can't be that bad," Zeke answered. "She's alive." And he felt that flutter in his chest again when he thought about Kira.

Zeke turned to look Den and noticed the dark rings under his eyes, the five o'clock shadow forming. He looked like he was falling apart slowly from the pressure. His hands shook. Zeke glanced at his band and noticed the lack of money. His first instinct was to get angry. He wanted to shake Den, to ask him what he was doing gambling again. But then Kira stirred and his head snapped back to her lying on the bed.

"I'm glad you saved her," Den said.

"Which time?" Zeke held back a pleased smile. "The time in the courtyard, the gauntlet, or when I found her in the trunk?"

Den closed his eyes and pinched the bridge of his nose. "All of the above. I never imagined she'd be this much trouble."

"All humans are."

"Remind me the next time I see one, to stay far away."

"This one has given us enough trouble that I think you've learned your lesson. So what's the plan?"

"We leave. It's obvious that we can no longer stay here. You and me, we stick to our plan and I train you. I've settled my debt with Remus, gave him everything I owe, and arranged for a place for us to hide out and get supplies."

Guilt rocked Zeke for a minute. Den hadn't gambled it away.

"What about her?" Zeke asked without looking at the bed.

"Not our problem."

"What do you mean 'not our problem'?" For the first time in a very long time he felt afraid. "This isn't like you, Den. How about we buy her from Remus." Zeke's breathing became ragged with panic.

"Too risky. The Underlords have sent two summons for her. I've... I've conveniently not told Remus about their summons. It's too late. We need to separate ourselves from her now before they come."

Zeke's hands clenched into fists. Anger boiled in him. "No," he growled.

"Why not? She'll distract them, and then we continue on with our plan. It's a good plan."

"Because I said NO!" Zeke hadn't meant to yell.

Den's face turned red, and then he looked at Kira. His eyes widened when he made the connection. "I see. So that's how it's going to be now."

Zeke could only watch as his friend discovered his weakness, and he didn't like the look in his eyes. He saw a flicker of greed and power flash across his face, and he noticed the small smile that crept across his lips. Now Den had more power over him. He wanted to cuss, throw something, but he held it together and remained silent. Because at that moment, he needed Den on his side, more than he needed Kira.

When Den said nothing, Zeke shifted uncomfortably. "You don't know what they're capable of. Not like I do." Zeke moved away from the hospital bed and toward the door, trying to put as much distance as he could between Kira and himself. As if by doing that he could protect her from his friend.

"You're right. I don't. Because you won't tell me everything!" Den snapped. "Our goal was to get you to the championship, a crack at the Labyrinth. Has that changed?"

Zeke swallowed. "No, but she comes with us."

Den spun and looked back at Kira lying on the bed. "She's dead weight now. She's a liability."

"We'll keep her as back up…for me." He hoped Den would believe that was the only reason he wanted her. "We won't have Warrick once we leave."

"Zeke," Den was wavering.

"You know I'm right. I won't leave here without her."

"Fine, but you need to come up with a way to get Remus to release her before the Olympus Tower comes to collect her. And until then we need someone to guard her from Remus."

"I can—"

"No. You stay far away from her." Den pointed his finger at him.

"Then who…Chaz?" Zeke asked.

Den snorted. "Not him, werecats are fickle. I wouldn't trust him as far as I can throw him. Besides, did you see how many freedom tokens he had today? We'll get Alice, since she's the one who found her. She'll be the best to watch her. No one will even know she's here."

"I agree." Zeke nodded. If it hadn't been for Alice, he may not have found Kira in time. He knew that the ghost girl had no love for Remus or his runners. She'd followed Kira that day because she felt a connection with her. Because Alice was at one time just like Kira. Human.

"We move tonight. With or without her." Den spun on his heels but turned back in warning. "And you can't be seen here anymore. Leave."

Zeke looked back at Kira and knew Den was right. If the Underlords were interested in her, then they'd be coming for her soon. And he needed to stay far away from both the Underlords and Kira…for now.

***

When Kira awoke for the first time and realized she was in the infirmary she cried—a deep, aching cry, even though she was too weak to make much noise. She'd hoped it was all a dream.

She heard a girl's gasp, but when she looked around saw only a plume of smoke. All through the night, as Kira slipped in and out of consciousness, she thought she saw someone sitting close to her bed and watching over her. But every time she turned her head to look, the girl was gone.

Her only evidence was the soft billowing wisp of smoke and an empty chair, which sat a little too close to the bed.

With the sheet over her head, Kira stared at the outline of the chair, barely discernible through the cotton. She would wait all day if she had to.

Kira's body hurt everywhere; not one inch of her body *didn't* feel bruised or sore. Who rescued her? And did they run her over with a car? Because that's what it felt like. When no one appeared in the chair, Kira did her best to slow her breathing, trying to feign sleep.

There it was—the sound she had been waiting for—a puff. She could have sworn she smelled lavender. The chair creaked. What should she say?

"I know you're there." Kira spoke softly through the sheet. "You can stop hiding."

"You sure?" The soft voice sounded so youthful and insecure that she immediately pegged the girl as a child. "He didn't want you to be alone in case someone else tried to hurt you."

Kira felt tired. "Who?"

"Den. I saw them chase you and what happened with the car. I found the zeke. He's the one who got you out of the trunk. The horse doctor pumped your stomach and gave you an antidote based on what cheetah said were the poisons. He asked me to watch over you in case someone else came." She rocked on the chair and pointed to Kira's wrist. "I saw your band. Someone stole your winnings. That's really sad." The voice sounded scared.

"How can they do that? Can't we do something about it?" Kira's fingers closed into an angry fist above the sheet.

"No. The witch won't have your winnings anymore. She'd have transferred them evenly among her coven members to hide it. To get it back you'd have to take them all on. It's not worth it. And you wouldn't survive."

"Does that happen a lot? Stealing of freedom tokens?"

She nodded her head. "Yes, it does. But people usually just turn around and steal from others to make it up, or from the dead."

"I wouldn't do that. I'm not like that." Kira pulled the sheet from her head and stared at the speaker. She was right; her guardian was a young girl, barely twelve years old. Strawberry gold hair spilled down her back, and she had intense green eyes. She wore overall shorts and a plaid shirt rolled up at the sleeves.

How or why this girl was watching over her, Kira couldn't figure out. But then again, she wasn't really a normal little girl, was she? "What's your name?"

"Alice." Her face lit up in a smile.

Kira rolled her eyes.

"And I know who you are." Alice leaned forward in her chair eagerly. "Everyone knows who you are. You're Kira, the human who killed Creeper and Bogeyman, and you survived the gauntlet. You're famous."

"I wouldn't say that."

She shook her head, "No, you have a whole fan club already."

"Oh yeah? Where were they when I was getting locked in a trunk and robbed?"

The smile slipped from Alice's face, and she bit her lip, refusing to make eye contact. In another puff of smoke she was gone, her chair empty. Kira reached forward and waved her hand over the chair, but it passed through air. This was nuts.

She laid back down on the bed and waited. For what, she wasn't sure. What seemed like hours but was probably only moments later, Warrick stepped into the room. His back was stiff and his bedside manner was odd. He checked her vitals but barely spoke to her.

"What's your problem?" Kira snarled at him after he jabbed her stomach painfully.

"You're my problem."

"I have no idea what you are talking about." She slapped his hand away from her.

Warrick stiffened and leaned away, as if the very touch of her hand on his arm offended him. What? Only a few days ago, he had been the one to try and take her into the city to "prepare" her for the race.

Now he acted like he didn't care.

He turned to grab something out of his medicine pouch and what she saw across his back made her stomach turn. Warrick's smooth skin was covered in angry red welts. Someone had taken a whip to his back, and the centaur hadn't been able to reach all of the wounds and treat himself. She could see a salve had been spread on the lower ones, but the upper welts were severely neglected.

"What happened? Who would do something like that?" Warrick wouldn't look at her. She finally started to understand his aloofness, his anger. It wasn't necessarily directed at her. It was because of her.

"It's because you healed me, isn't it?"

His tail flicked and he gazed down at his hooves.

"You got in trouble for it."

He nodded. "Remus had forbidden me from helping you, but it goes against my code. No one has the right to stop a healer from healing." His voice burned with conviction.

"Give me the salve, and I'll help treat your back."

Warrick backed away, his voice an angry whisper. "Don't. Just listen to what I have to say—and don't react. You don't have much time."

She closed her mouth and listened.

"You're all over the news. Human surviving the gauntlet. You're gaining attention from many factions, both the Pro-Human and Pro-Beast." He was still whispering. "It's caused a bit of an uproar over the last three days."

"Three days? Wait. How long have I been in the infirmary?"

"You've been in and out of it for quite a while. The Underlords have sent two emissaries from Olympus Tower requesting your presence. Which isn't good."

"What do I do?" Kira asked. "You should've let me die."

"That is not your destiny," Warrick spoke in clipped tones. "Three times now, you have beaten your death. I don't know how long you can continue to run from it, but I will do everything in my power to keep you alive for whatever purpose fate has for you."

He glanced back at the partially open door and tensed. "No more talking." He moved away, and Kira saw a shadow move outside the door.

When Warrick finished with her examination, he placed a small plastic cup on the nightstand with an oblong white pill.

"What is that?" She eyed the pill with distrust.

"Wintergreen and clove. That, my dear unfortunate girl, is all you get." He moved away from the bed and replaced the solitary chair. He turned to leave. The door moved slightly as someone, probably their observer, tried to close it before he could get there.

Fear ran up and down her spine. She didn't want to be alone.

"Warrick, please," she said softly. It must have been the please that broke him, because his shoulders slumped and his head drooped. "I know I've been an ungrateful jerk, and rude…and obnoxious." It was working because he turned his soft brown eyes upon her. "Please, tell me what is going to happen to me now."

"I don't know, but I believe the fates may be on your side."

Kira sighed. She didn't believe in any of this fate stuff. She dropped her head back onto the pillow and tried to blink away tears of self-pity. It was fine.

Kira let the silence fill the room.

Warrick seemed done, but he was wasting time before leaving. She hadn't known the centaur long, but she felt a fondness for the equine doctor. So much to consider.

"Why did you have me give Zeke chocolate?"

Warrick looked over his shoulder at the empty chair and waved. "Because you needed more friends." He stepped through the door. Just before it shut, he ducked back in and whispered, "Good thing too, because it helped in the gauntlet. You never know where help will come from."

Kira stared at the door for a moment, and then back at the chair. Could he see her visitor, even though she couldn't?

That was all she needed, someone else to feel indebted to. She didn't even know who Alice was, and now she owed the girl her life. And she owed Zeke for saving her life twice. What if he wanted her life in exchange? Her life was getting suckier by the minute.

Still, they'd done what they could—more than they should've—to keep her alive. Kira had too much of her father's military honor to just turn her back on all they'd done for her. Sure, she could be a pain, but usually because of self-preservation.

She'd never gotten to go to high school, but even on the streets it was safer in numbers. Easier to scour for food or pick pockets if someone played the decoy. Maybe she could use some of those tricks down here to survive. She needed to make some kind of alliance down here. From what little she could see of little Alice, she wouldn't have been Kira's first choice for an ally.

Twenty-One

No one else came to visit her, which only made Kira even more irritated. She glanced at the door for the tenth time.

A soft giggle came from the area of the chair again. A moment later the chair filled with Alice's small form, sitting with her knees pulled up to her chest. Her green eyes smiled mischievously.

"He's not going to come," Alice said.

"Why not?" Kira snapped, assuming Alice meant Den again.

"Because he said he couldn't come back. For your own safety he needs to pretend you aren't important. Until he's ready."

"How do you know? Why would you say that?"

"He was here when you were first unconscious. I hid so he didn't know I was here. He looked really, really sad," Alice whispered the last bit and lowered her head.

"I don't think Den would be sad—more like ticked."

Alice shook her head, "Not him, the zeke."

"What?" Kira tried to imagine Zeke in her room watching her while she was sleeping. The tug of a smile started at the corner of her mouth. "So you really rescued me with Zeke, huh?"

Alice bobbed her head excitedly.

"Why would you do that? You don't know me."

"It's the same thing Warrick said. We need to make strong friends to survive. I want to help you."

The girl seemed so earnest and hopeful. Kira chewed the inside of her lip, weighing her options. Her decision would impact—not only her but— the young and naïve girl.

"Sure. Why not?" Kira stuck her hand out and waited for Alice to shake it in agreement, but she didn't take it. Instead, in another puff of smoke, the girl disappeared from the chair and reappeared on the bed next to Kira, giving her an all-encompassing hug. Alice practically crawled into Kira's lap and buried her head into her shoulder, like a small puppy seeking solace. Except that where Alice's skin touched Kira, she felt a slight pressure and a breeze.

Kira wasn't prepared for the close contact, but instinct made her wrap an arm around the girl. It felt so foreign to be holding someone, offering comfort after years of neglect. But at the same time it felt right.

In that one moment, this small girl had found a chink in Kira's armor. Kira, hardened by life on the street, knew right then she would do everything she could to protect the child.

Tears started to form in her eyes, and her heart ached from the pain and regret of all she'd been missing in her lonely life. That one action gave Kira, even though it was a small one, a reason to live.

"I've got to go. It's almost time." The ghost disappeared without giving her anymore answers and didn't return. Kira tried to get out of bed, but she was too weak. Her body was still healing, and she was wracked with coughs.

***

Kira ached, still. Her body felt like it had been through torture—it basically had. She'd been asleep for only an hour when Olympus Tower guards in white uniforms burst into her hospital room.

"That's her." The guard pointed, and they hauled her out of bed.

"What's going on?" Kira asked the guard twisting her right arm. "Where are you taking me?" She tried to see through his reflective facemask.

"You've been summoned by the Underlords. Since you've ignored those summons, you are under arrest," the shorter guard answered.

"What? No, I didn't know. I've obviously been ill!" Kira tried to explain.

The guard on her left yelled. "Silence."

As they dragged her through the compound, she saw Remus shouting at a third Olympus Guard. Her legs burned, and her head pounded from the jostling.

"This can't be. I own that human. You can't just march in here and take it from me."

"Are you disobeying the orders of the Underlords?" the guard challenged.

Remus's face paled. "Why no, but I—"

The men stopped suddenly, and Kira swung forward, jarred. Their gloved hands squeezed her biceps until she thought she'd lose circulation. They held Kira a few feet from Remus, while the third guard tapped his tablet.

"I'll have to report your insubordination to Hermes."

Sweat broke out on Remus's forehead, and he steadied himself against the wall. "But it's just a human. What could they want with a human girl?"

"Who are you to question them?"

"I didn't mean—I don't—This is the first I've heard of any summons."

The guard speaking to Remus lifted his visor. The manticore's mouth pulled back to reveal his sharp teeth.

"Do you deny their direct order?" His scorpion tail arched above them, the barb glistening with poison.

Remus's shoulders sagged. "No, no. Never. Bring it here. I'll release it right now."

The two guards with iron grip dragged Kira over to Remus, and the guard on her right yanked her arm up in front of him. He punched a few numbers into her brace, and she heard a beeping. Something powered down. Her tracker maybe? The guards quickly moved her away from Remus and toward a white van with the Olympus Tower on its side.

"I'll be expecting compensation." Remus smiled at the manticore. "That was one of my most prized fighters."

"Yet you'll receive none. After all, this is a gift, because you refused the gods."

"No, no. I told you. This is the first I've heard of the summons. I didn't know." He stomped his feet, and the guard beside her shook his head.

"Not my problem." The manticore waved at Remus, did an about face, and marched to the driver's side of the vehicle. The guards shoved Kira into the back and the two guards stepped up after her, slamming the door. The engine turned over and they drove off.

How could this day get any worse? She stared at the two guards. Maybe if she knew what kind of monsters they were, it'd be easier for her to calm herself down. Exhausted, head pounding, she laid her head against the side of the cage and prayed for swift healing while she tried to hold back the tears. She hadn't gotten to say goodbye. She'd just been taken.

They went over a rib-cage rattling bit of road. She coughed, and when she pulled her hands away, she saw a few spots of blood.

"What is that?" the guard hissed, finally talking to her. "Are you bleeding?"

"No," she lied, tucking her hands into her sleeves. She might be honest if they'd tell her what was going on.

The guard reached up and raised his visor, revealing his dark and familiar eyes. "Don't lie to me!"

"Zeke?" Kira gushed. She almost cried. The other guard lifted his visor, and Kira was greeted with Den's unshaven and tired face. "What? How?"

Den looked over his shoulder at Zeke, sitting just behind the driver. He kneeled next to her, leaned in close and whispered, "Listen, Kira. And listen well."

She rolled her eyes. She didn't just forgive and forget.

Den frowned and clenched his jaw at her obvious disdain. "Remus wants you dead."

"He could have killed me any time he wanted in the infirmary. I was right there—weak." she whispered back.

Den's eyes lit. He glanced over his shoulder at the Zeke and a look passed between them. When he turned back, he spoke quickly, as if he knew his time was short. "We came up with a plan."

"I came up with a plan." Zeke answered, his voice filled with tension.

"What Remus wants, Remus gets," Den said. "The best thing for you is to get as far away from both of them—Remus and the Underlords—as possible. So we're leaving."

"Leaving?"

"Yeah. He doesn't know that we scammed him yet, but he will figure it out soon. That means we've got targets on our back now. The Underlords did send for you, and--yes—you can't hide from them for long." He wasn't telling her the whole truth.

"So am I free?" She looked at her bracer, and Den shook his head.

"Technically, you're a free Underlander. But remember, Kira, you can't leave. The band can't come off. The Underlords are still searching for you, and Remus will hunt you too."

Zeke's dark eyes found Kira's in the truck bed. She stirred uncomfortably under his stare. Kira swallowed and pretended to be fascinated by the frayed edging of her cuff less jacket. As hard as she tried not to, she was becoming very fascinated with him.

The truck entered one of the tunnels. They were traveling in complete darkness except for the truck's headlights. The time stretched on and on—no one said a thing for close to twenty minutes.

"Where are we going?"

"You'll see when we get there."

After a few more minutes, Den reached down and pounded three times. The truck pulled over, and they all hopped out onto the side of the road. Den began to pull off a giant decal revealing an Olympus Electric and Plumbing logo. The guys changed out of their uniforms and dropped them into a deep crevasse a few yards down away from the road.

Zeke spoke to the manticore and gave him a quick hug, then they watched the van drive off.

"Let's go." Den said. He and Zeke each pulled a flashlight out of his backpack, and they started off down the road.

"How did you do that?" Kira asked. "Stage the breakout, get the Olympus Guard uniforms."

"Ask Zeke." Den kept walking.

She turned to look at Zeke, and he shrugged. "I've got resources. It's safer for you if you don't know more than that."

Even if she wanted to press for more information, she couldn't. Exhaustion was overtaking her, and she was lucky to keep putting one foot in front of the other.

Kira's coughing broke the tense silence. Loud racking coughs ripped through her chest, and she turned her head into her sleeve, doing her best to keep quiet and hide the blood spots from Den.

He grabbed her elbow and shone his flashlight on the small specks of blood splattered across her jacket cuff. "Kira, anything Remus or the Underlords use to track can smell blood. You're going to get killed or eaten before we even have a chance to get there." In seconds, he ripped the cuff off her jacket and shoved the blood-splattered denim into his cargo pants pocket, shooting a worried look toward Zeke.

Zeke's nostrils flared, but he closed his eyes and turned his head away painfully.

They had only been travelling for thirty minutes when a voice came out of the darkness. "Remus knows you betrayed him. The real Olympus Guards just showed up to collect her. He's very, very angry." Kira smelled lavender, and Alice appeared suddenly beside her.

When he turned, the light of Den's flashlight on her blurred the edges of her white dress. Den cussed under his breath.

"He's been released." Alice's already pale cheeks were stark white with fear. She pointed back the way they'd come.

"One of the hellhounds?" Den asked. "We can handle it."

"No." Alice shook her head. "Dip."

"Go!" Den grabbed Kira's jacket and pulled her after him. "Run!"

"No!" Alice flew toward them and yanked on Kira's bloodied jacket, pulling it frantically. "It has blood on it. Give it to *me*. Give me yours too." The young ghost continued her panicked tugging, and Kira slid her arms out. The jacket flew from her arms. Zeke, suddenly beside them, removed his outer shirt. Den took off his leather jacket and pulled the strip of her bloodied cuff from his pocket.

"Go," Alice whispered, the word loud in the dangerous darkness. But—what was Dip exactly?

Den pulled out his knife and sliced his hand, dripping a few drops onto his jacket before handing it over.

"Good. I'll lay a false trail for the beast." She started to disappear, but Den called out to her.

"Thank you, Alice."

She slowly reappeared. "Just remember me, please. Don't forget about me." She was gone, and the fragrant aroma of her presence evaporated.

"Come. We have to move." Den demanded they follow him.

"Wait," Kira said. "Will she be okay? What's after us?"

Den shook his head in frustration. "Dip. A demon dog that lives off the blood of those he hunts."

"But Alice is a ghost, so she should be fine right?" Kira needed one of them to allay her fears.

"Dip is a *demon*." He gave her a look as if that explained everything. Kira didn't understand the connection, but Den was only concerned about getting them as far away from their current location as possible.

Kira looked to Zeke for an answer. He whispered, "Yes, she is a ghost and for the most part can't be hurt."

"What are neither one of you telling me?" She was too tired to run. Her head felt as if someone was playing dodgeball inside her skull.

"Ghosts can only be destroyed by someone of the supernatural realm, like angels…" He trailed off unwilling to say the rest.

"And demons," Kira finished, uneasy. Why would this ghost girl sacrifice so much for them? It didn't make sense.

"Kira," Zeke reached forward and touched her shoulder. She felt an electric shock at his touch. "She's fast, she's good, and she's old." Kira stared up at him in confusion. "Which means she's strong."

"Then why hasn't she left the compound? She's a ghost. Couldn't she leave anytime?" Kira was already losing her breath.

"She can't." Zeke stepped quickly over a boulder and turned to look back at her. "She died there. She has to return to that place frequently so that she can remember her death. The longer she's away, the weaker she becomes, and the more she fades. And if anyone forgets her—including herself—she'll disappear for good and not have the strength to return.

"If the demon gets to her in this state, she'll never come back."

It made sense. Alice's parting words—they were said out of fear. A pang stabbed Kira in her chest, and she stopped on the trail. She couldn't protect the girl, and she had promised herself she'd try. This was exactly why it was so hard to care for people, why she hardened her heart against feeling anything. Because everyone she loved or cared for eventually died or betrayed her.

"Kira, come on," Zeke pleaded.

Kira glared at Den as she hurried breathlessly along behind him and knew it to be true. Traitor. He'd let the girl go off to face the demon alone. Even if they had a plan, Kira couldn't help but feel resentment towards Den.

He looked back. "You can't save everyone." He must have read her expression.

"You can try," she snapped.

"Not overnight. Right now, I just need to focus on saving you and him." He gestured for them to follow him as he turned into an even darker tunnel.

Kira's eyes adjusted fast but not before she stumbled. Zeke reached out through the blackness and touched her hand. She pulled back, startled by the coldness of his skin. Somewhere between life and death. Kira realized it probably seemed like she didn't trust him. She slowed and reached behind her until she found his arm. She felt past his elbow. And this time, she gripped his hand and held on.

A flash in his pupils said she'd surprised him. It almost made her pull away, but instead, she pressed her lips together and gave his hand an affirming squeeze.

As soon as they stepped out of the darkness of the tunnel, they were on the outskirts of the city. She wasn't sure why, if they were hiding, they'd go to a densely populated area. Maybe so many different scents would throw off whatever hunted them. Maybe hiding in plain sight was a favorite tactic of Den's. Either way, better than cowering in a tunnel somewhere, waiting to be attacked.

She doubted Den ever cowered.

"Why the city?" She stumbled, and Zeke slowed to wait for her to catch her breath.

Den didn't wait. "More scents, and easier to pay for silence," Den pulled his cloak over his head, hiding his identity.

Paying for silence. That was smart. How easy would it be to disappear? Especially if she was on her own.

Landmarks were starting to look familiar, mostly because she used Olympus Tower as her point of reference. When they came to a steel grain silo, Den tossed his duffel bag on the ground and unlocked the door. He disappeared inside. From within, they heard an electric buzz, followed by a pop. Den muttered something, and eventually, a flood of light spilled forth.

The last thing Kira wanted was to be trapped—even with Zeke and Den. Sure, it was somewhere new, but she still wasn't free until she could get the band off. All they had to do was activate it again and they'd find her. Kira tried to back up, but she bumped into Zeke, an immobile wall. Too tired to fight him, Kira took her first tentative steps into the building.

"Home sweet home," Den said as he closed an electrical box and came to stand near them, his hands on his hips. His face beamed with pride.

"You should fire your decorator," Kira joked. The vastness surprised her, but it didn't keep the room from feeling like a large round prison cell. More than anything, she just wanted freedom.

Still, the place wasn't bare. Off to one side stood an old wood-burning stove, and a few crates sat around an old card table. She looked up and saw holes in the roof and a metal ladder running up the inside of the building.

Probably not quite as secure as they needed it to be.

"Well, it will get there." Den clapped his hands and eyed the place excitedly.

Zeke immediately went for the ladder and started to climb the interior wall of the old grain bin. Someone before had added steel crossbeams and wood floors for more usable living space on one side of the silo. Ropes hung across the space with lights dangling from them. It seemed Zeke was aiming to crawl to the light that had burnt out. He shimmied down the pole and reached for the old bulb.

Den went back outside, returned with his duffel, and dropped it on the floor. Dust rose up into the air.

Kira tried to fan away the dirt cloud and sneezed. It burned, but thankfully, she didn't see any blood.

"What now?" She rubbed her boot across the dry ground and discovered actual cement underneath all the dirt. The silo just needed a lot of sweeping and mopping. But what was Den going to do with this place? Did he intend for them to stay long?

"Nothing right now. Just stay here while I get some supplies and see if we've been followed."

She just nodded, relieved that she had time to get some rest. Once the stress-induced adrenaline wore off, Kira's exhaustion slammed back into her. She moved to lean against a wall.

The silo door closed behind them. Kira stared at the door, knowing freedom wasn't very far away. It almost gave her hope for a minute.

Zeke seemed preoccupied with walking across the beams. He enjoyed the dangerous balancing act with such grace that she was jealous at his acrobatic ability. He turned, jumped up to another beam, and pulled himself up another level.

Kira wanted to breathe air that hadn't been trapped in this vault for months. She casually made her way to the silo door and reached for the metal handle. Something large dropped in front of her and blocked her. She jumped.

"Where do you think you're going?" Zeke said stiffly. Wasn't he just as anxious as she was to leave the prison?

"Do you ever think about running? Really breaking free? Wouldn't it be great to just leave—both of us? We'd just need to get these off." She held up her band.

"And go where exactly?"

"Home. My home." The words felt hollow out loud. Home should refer to somewhere warm, loving, a place where she felt safe and secure. She didn't have one of those. Her childhood home was gone, and all she had left were the streets of Portland. If she got away, where *would* she go?

Zeke laughed. "Back to the surface? Do you really think my kind is welcome there? Once someone sees me go berserk, it's all over."

Is that what he called it—berserk?

"Your doctors would dissect me, study me, and regenerate me until I resembled nothing more than the walking corpses in your movies. It's happened before to others. That's no life for me up there."

"And this is death for me down here. I have as much chance of survival down here as you do up there. I don't belong." She tried to push past him, but Zeke grabbed her wrist.

"I'm sorry, I can't let you go. It's too dangerous out there with Dip on your tail."

Kira pulled her arm from his grasp and huffed. "Maybe I'd like those chances better than to stay here as a prisoner."

Zeke narrowed his eyes. "You could stay and help with our plans. After all, you know nothing of what we're trying to do."

"Your plans?" she pondered the words. Suddenly, it all made sense. "Den knew you before the slave market didn't he?"

"Yes, I was sent there as punishment for a crime. But Den and I go way back, and we planned for him to buy me. Now our goal is to compete—to get to the Labyrinth."

"Why were you imprisoned there in the first place?"

Zeke's mouth lifted into a mischievous smile. "For trying to break into the Labyrinth. I got caught."

She couldn't believe it. "What's the big deal about the Labyrinth?"

He got a far-off look in his eyes. "I think the answers are inside."

"Answers to what?"

He became really quiet, and she knew she probably needed to let it drop. "So why'd you protect me in the courtyard?"

"You needed help." He shrugged as if it wasn't a big deal.

"And why'd you helped me cross the finish line?"

"Den asked me to help you cross, although you did pretty well on your own. You had 50-1 odds. We're team Den."

"Sound like Team Zen to me."

"What's a Zen?"

"What I'm calling your bromance. Den combined with Zeke. Or you could be team Deke."

Zeke actually laughed. It was warm, freeing, and she smiled.

When Zeke stopped laughing he became serious for a moment. "He's not a saint, you know. You don't know him like I do. Just…try to make the best of it. Being team Zeken is…bigger than us."

"Now that's just dumb." Kira snorted at his attempt to combine all three names. As dumb as the name was, it sounded right to be a part of something.

The weight of the trip had more than caught up with her. Her body screamed to sleep, to rest. To close her eyes and focus on not feeling. She trudged to the far wall and sat against it, pulling her knees up to her chest. The dust got her coughing again, but this time she noticed there was less blood. Which was good. Still, it was painful.

She dropped her head to her knees and closed her eyes, trying to imagine herself in a better situation. Another coughing fit rattled her, and she wiped at her face with her sleeve.

This level of exhaustion was new. It made her crazy emotional, brought on tears of frustration that brimmed in her eyes. She worried about Alice out there with that demon hunting them. She wondered what the Underlords wanted her for. But she tried to think on what Zeke said, focus on the big picture. To do that, alliances would be crucial—and not just with Alice. She needed to build trust with these guys. They had just saved her, again. So she'd give Team Zeken, or whatever, a chance.

Something fell from above and dangled precariously close to her body. Kira jumped back and smacked her head on the silo wall. Her brain practically vibrated. "What the..?" A can of food had dropped thirty feet from above and was dangling in front of her. She really didn't think she'd get used to that.

"Come." He beckoned up the ladder.

Now, more than curious, she climbed the ladder and very carefully stepped onto the third-level floor. The two levels below didn't cover but a portion of the silo—maybe fifteen feet across. She was pretty high up, so she hugged the wall and stayed away from the drop.

Zeke was walking across the beam above her. He lowered a mass of rope and canvas from it. It spun slowly in front of her, and then Zeke climbed down the ropes like Spiderman. He jumped to her floor, a grin of triumph on his face.

"Here." He gestured to the tangled mass.

Kira scrunched her brow in confusion. But as he pulled the ropes and canvas apart, it unrolled into a shape she quickly recognized. Zeke had crafted a makeshift hammock.

"It's better than sleeping on the floor. I think the farther we can keep you away from the dirt, the quicker you'll heal."

It was beautiful. Thoughtful. The nicest gift anyone had given her in…well, years. She was so overcome with emotion that she stared dumfounded at the hammock. Zeke offered his hand and helped pull her up. He held it steady and helped her to sit in it, to find her center of gravity. Kira laid down and felt her body sway back and forth in the hammock. The gentle rocking movement was comforting.

The thought and effort he'd put into it overwhelmed her. Finally, the dam broke. She cried.

Zeke looked at her confused. "Do you not like it? I know it could have been better, but it's the only material I found. There's not much here, as you can see."

"No, it's perfect." She wiped away her tears and gave him a smile. It felt odd to do such a simple thing as smile with happiness. She tried to remember the last time she had felt this happy and grateful—but she couldn't. "Thank you."

Zeke returned her smile, and it hit her hard.

Her smile faltered. Something stirred within her chest and beat wildly, not out of fear.

The hammock slowed. Zeke lay down next to it, and she felt the pressure of his hand on the side as he pushed her gently. Was a zombie really rocking her to sleep? Would he eat her if she nodded off? No. If he wanted to eat her, he would have done it already.

This was just a new feeling, a confusing feeling, something she hadn't felt in a very long time. Trust.

She didn't know what to make of it.

She stared upward through the hole in the roof. She could almost imagine seeing stars through the hole, but she knew there were no stars down here. More than likely it was the reflection of diamonds or precious stones in the rocky ceiling. Things like this would catch her by surprise sometimes. Remind her how much she missed the surface, the air, the cool breeze, the sounds of the traffic.

"Have you ever seen stars?"

"It's been a very long time since I've seen the sky," he said. "It was very beautiful, but night was nothing compared to your sunrise. Seeing that giant ball of fire rise across the horizon, and watching your world slowly awaken to its call was the most breathtaking thing I've ever seen.

But the last time I saw it, I couldn't stay long. I felt overwhelmed, exposed, and it became uncomfortable to stay without feeling a pressure in my chest."

"Hmm. I wonder why?"

"I think your kind call it agoraphobia. The freshness of the air makes us a little sick, and it takes a bit to adapt."

She could understand. Her first few days had been like that. But after a while, the lack of natural light and the deep earthy and musty smell that had bothered her faded. She hardly noticed it anymore. She was adapting.

And that scared her.

Twenty-Two

Alice flew as fast as she could, carrying the bloodied clothes of her new friends. She'd backtracked toward the compound, hoping to lay the scent trail so Dip could follow her. The closer she got to the compound, the stronger she felt.

A tall man walked on the path right as it narrowed. She had no choice—she rushed right through him, backpack and all.

"Yeow!" The man with spotted hair yelled. Her cold presence probably felt like an ice bath to him. But Alice didn't have time to worry about it.

She heard a growl in the distance, followed by a long, haunting howl.

Dip.

He smelled the blood.

He was on the hunt.

And if she didn't get the blood down on the trail and away from her, he wouldn't care who he mauled. She couldn't pass through any solid surface with the clothes she was holding, so she'd have to lay the trail the hard way. There. The side spur that forked off the main tunnel was where she needed to smear the blood.

Her hands shook as she flew down the smaller tunnel. She didn't know these tunnels. She didn't like to stray this far away from home.

A loud bark echoed off the tunnel walls. Alice wanted to drop the clothes and run for her undead life. But she couldn't. She hadn't made any headway. If she failed, Dip would easily overtake her friends.

Alice sang a song from her childhood in her head as she took another turn and ended up winding her way back to the beginning of the tunnel system. Light shone—it sounded like Dip had already entered the tunnels and was somewhere behind her.

Alice made a dash for the exit. She pressed Kira's jacket close to her heart and felt a moment of pride. She had done it. She had helped her human friend. Her undead life would not be in vain. She'd never be forgotten.

Alice's head had just cleared the tunnel when sharp demon teeth punctured her leg and Dip's powerful jaws clamped down on her. The pain! The heat! She turned as Dip dragged her back down into the tunnel. Disappear! Disappear!

It was no use. She couldn't apparate when he had a hold of her.

She screamed. The demon dog's teeth began to shred through her ethereal form. It burned her like fire, like it was raking coals across her soul. She tried to fly upward. Her hands scratched and scraped at the tunnel ceiling as she pulled against his grip.

He released her, and she clawed her way to the entrance. She felt Dip's evil breath on her neck as he slowly stalked her. He was toying with her now, letting her crawl away. She whimpered. Her body flickered in the light, beginning to fade. The demon's bite was killing her.

The tall man with the backpack! There he was again. His face grew white with fear when he saw the demon dog behind her. But she saw determination in his eyes too. She remembered his name now.

Chaz.

He shifted into cheetah form, and she heard his feline hiss. He was going to challenge the demon dog.

"No!" she cried out. "Help them." Alice tossed the bloodied jacket toward cheetah. Chaz leaned down and sniffed the jacket. He shook his head and eyed the demon. He growled again, his fur standing on end, his back arched high as he took another threatening step toward the demon dog.

"It's too late for me!" Alice cried, tears running down her face. "Help Kira. Save them." Chaz turned and looked at the path she had flown down, and she knew he'd be able to find them. If anyone could outrun the Dip, he could.

She felt warm drool on the back of her neck. Dip was watching her fade away. She wouldn't give him the satisfaction of facing him in fear and sadness. It was over. She had done well.

Chaz picked up the bloodied jacket in his mouth and took off running.

There. Now she could face him. She'd seen to her friends' safety. Alice turned over to look into Dip's red demon eyes.

"I'm not afraid of death."

Dip's mouth opened wide.

Twenty-Three

"Wake up, sleeping ugly." Zeke poked her in the side.

Kira groaned. She couldn't move. Or at least she didn't want to. How in the world had she slept so soundly swinging in a hammock suspended in an underground grain silo next to a freaking zombie? She rolled over and noticed Zeke hadn't moved from his spot.

"Don't you mean Sleeping Beauty, like the fairytales?"

"We don't believe in fairytales."

"Why not?"

"Because there are no such thing as happy endings. In our version, the princess—well, she's not beautiful. She's quite ugly, which is a compliment for our kind."

"Are you saying calling me ugly was your way of paying me a compliment?"

"Uh….no?"

See, with girls, there never was really a safe answer when you just called someone ugly. She studied his panicked face as he laid there on the floor and decided to let it go. "Did you really stay there all night?"

"Yep." He didn't seem bothered by it.

"Do you ever sleep?"

"Not usually. Sometimes I can, but what's the point? I don't dream."

"Then why wake me?"

"Because Den is back." He sat up, dusted off his back, and moved to the edge. His feet hit the floor level seconds before Den walked through. He must have great hearing to hear him that far off.

But why had he moved away so quickly? Was he embarrassed to be seen so close to her? Was he was hiding something from her?

She couldn't believe how much better she felt this morning. Renewed even. Maybe all of the adrenaline from yesterday helped. What had happened with Alice? She hoped to see her face soon.

***

Den burned with fury over the news he'd picked up in the city. It seemed like they'd caused more problems than they'd solved. He shoved open the silo door and announced loudly, "We've gone and done it now." He dropped the box of supplies and looked around.

Kira swung in a makeshift hammock.

Zeke was standing pretty far away from the girl. A little too far away. And she kept casting him awkward glances. Yeah, Zeke liked her, and was trying to hide it from him.

Zeke came forward and started to sort through the stuff in the box. "What happened?" He didn't seem at all interested. He could have been asking instead what was on TV.

"The rumble last night. It was a massacre." The most recent game had cost so, so many lives.

Zeke paused and glanced up at Kira, his face a blank mask. "How many?" He asked the silent question that only they knew. How many were drafted as well.

"Too many. There's never been that many that fast." Den answered. "The Gamblers' Market was empty when I went by. Everyone had been ordered to the event—old and young. By decree of the Underlords."

"You need to let me compete." Zeke turned and grabbed Den's shirt front. Den's body thudded against the wall.

Den could have easily fought back, but he stuck to his wits and spoke calmly. "You can be sure Remus will send his best to try and take you down. Especially now, because of her. I think we have to sit the televised ones out. Low profile. That's what. We can still win our way up, become a champion another way."

Zeke kept glancing the girl's way, but he didn't make any effort to include her in the conversation. "I can handle myself—doesn't matter the event, Den."

"Listen, you. You fight when I want you to fight. I don't want to blow your cover too soon. We need patience." Den slowly uncurled Zeke's fingers from his shirt.

"We need tokens."

A loud knock rang through the silo. Both males froze.

"You expecting company?" Zeke asked.

"No. If it was Alice, she'd just come through the wall." Den reached behind his neck, and pulled out the katana from its sheath. With slow, controlled movements, he slipped over to the door and pushed it open. Light spilled in, and the familiar form of Chaz stepped through.

In a flash Den had his sword at Chaz's throat.

"Hey, hey, I surrender!" Chaz's hands went straight up in the air. "Is that even sharp?" He gave Den a grin but it faltered. "I guess I could do with a bit of a shave, but not too much, kay?" He looked pretty beat up. Sported a couple cuts and bruises across his face, and a long cut on his shoulder.

"What do you want, Chaz?" Den dropped the sword, but he cut off the lycanthrope from entering the silo any further. Zeke moved so his body blocked Kira from Chaz's site.

"Your gang tried to poison Kira, which you know is against the rules."

"Wait, what?" Chaz's smile dropped. "No, that wasn't me. That was Holly and her coven—on Remus's orders. I'm not with them anymore. Actually"—he lifted his wrist—"I'm a Paladin. As of the rumble last night. And I'm positive Remus didn't intend to let me earn my freedom. So…I can't go back. No loyalties, no allies. Unless you're looking for one."

"I don't trust you," Zeke spoke up.

"I'm the one who smelled the poison, right?" Chaz looked around Zeke and tried to spot the girl. "Tell them, Kira. I could have kept my mouth shut and watched you keel over, but I didn't. I helped."

Den looked over to her and she nodded. "Yeah, he did save me."

Zeke stepped to the side so Kira could be part of the conversation. But he stayed close. "Doesn't answer our question. What are you doing here? How did you find us?"

Chaz grinned. "Easy." He looked over at Kira and winked. "I marked her with my scent."

"What? Ew!" Kira groaned and started patting her clothes.

"No you didn't," Zeke growled out. His patience was done.

Chaz swallowed and dropped his head to his chest. "The ghost girl."

Kira sat up. "Alice. Is she okay?"

Chaz shook his head. "No, she didn't make it. The demon dog got her. I'm sorry."

Den swore under his breath. He motioned for them to get going. "We have to go. Now. We can't stay here any longer. If he got her, he got a taste of our blood too. He won't stop until we're dead."

"You're wrong." Chaz tossed Kira's jacket and the rest of the bloodied clothes on the floor in front of them.

"You fool!" Den yelled. "You've led him right to our doorstep."

"No," Chaz turned and looked at Kira. "I killed him."

"Impossible." Den moved to the door to watch for the dog.

"I was there when the ghost girl died." Chaz looked sad, but then he squared his shoulders and met Den's eyes. "I took the bloodied clothes and got Dip off your trail. I avenged the girl, and then I made sure Remus's demon couldn't come after me either. I killed Dip."

"How?

Chaz looked a little unstable on his feet, but then he shrugged proudly and winked. "Dogs may be stronger than cats, but don't forget"—he tapped his head—"cats are smarter."

"How did you kill the demon dog?" Den repeated.

"I led him down into the salt pit. Surrounded by a circle of salt, a demon dog can be killed." He licked a wound on his shoulder. "Although getting that kind of salt in your wounds burns like the high heavens. But it was worth it." Chaz shrugged.

Huh. That was actually pretty brilliant.

Kira moved to get him some water.

Den finally let himself sit down. He held his katana across his lap. Zeke grabbed a few bandages from the supplies Den had gotten and gave them to Kira.

Chaz actually looked like he was going to start purring when her hands gently brushed his neck and she started to clean his wounds.

***

"Well, at least the salt will kill any bacteria," Kira said softly. Her hands worked slowly as she felt the weight of Alice's death like a lodestone around her neck. It was hard for her to swallow, to keep back the tears. She decided just not to fight them, crying silently.

Chaz butted her with his head, and she buried her fingers in his hair.

He stretched and closed his eyes. He probably would have gotten more comfortable if Zeke hadn't come over and started to bandage his cuts with a firmer hand.

"Easy there, boy," Chaz warned. "I'm a hero."

Chaz looked to her for approval. Zeke just seemed like he wanted to help speed up the process and get Chaz on his way. Finally, he left the bandaging to Kira and moved to stand by the wall.

Chaz sighed. "There's been a surge of new champions entered in this next event all of a sudden."

"That happens all the time," Den said, clearly impatient. "Especially after a devastating event like the gauntlet. Owners and trainers start buying out the Gamblers' Market. I went by and it was empty. They—"

Chaz swallowed. "Nope, these ones didn't come from the market. Pickings have been slow."

"Chaz, spit it out!" Zeke slammed his fist into the wall and left a large dent.

Kira jumped and looked at Zeke in confusion. Why did he seem so ungrateful? Chaz had just risked his life for them.

Chaz seemed unfazed. "They came from above!" He smiled and watched Den. "Ah, but I can tell by your reaction, you knew that already."

"What?" Kira asked and looked over at Den. That's why he was so mad when he stormed in. He knew and wasn't going to tell her.

Zeke figured it out, but she didn't.

"After the gauntlet, there was a surge on the market for humans, but there haven't been any. So a few parties have gone up and come back down with some. Supply and demand, you know? I wonder what made them want humans so bad." Chaz turned his head up at Kira and winked.

She dropped the bandage and it rolled across the floor.

"What about the ban?" Kira asked.

"It's been lifted," Chaz answered. "Not permanently, but it seems that they've okayed the abduction of humans for the games."

"What?" The horror of what happened to her washed back over her. Her kidnapping, her branding, her being sold on the market. She wouldn't wish it on anyone. And now, because of her knack at surviving, others had been taken and forced into the games. What was a spur of the moment, quick buck for Alpo and Vic, had now become the thing.

"How many were entered?" Kira was numb.

"Two in the rumble last night, and they didn't make it. Five are signed up for next week's already. I looked at the roster." He let his hand brush against his pant leg. "Remus ordered Holly to go up to get him one as well after he lost you. It's why I left. I wouldn't do it."

Kira looked at Den and pointed at him. "You have to stop this."

"The ball's in motion. We can't stop it," he answered. "We just have to wait for it to die down."

She looked at Chaz. "So where are you going to go now?"

"I thought maybe you could use a sponsor. I can coach you through some of the smaller events. The ring maybe." He gestured between them. "We'd make a great team."

Kira's cheeks warmed. Flattered at the offer.

Zeke stepped in front of Kira. "She'll get back to you."

"Hey…wait," Kira argued. "He helped us."

"You already have a team." Zeke stared at her. "Remember?" His dark eyes pleaded with her, and she couldn't help but look between the two of them. How did Chaz and Zeke both want her to be on their team? It was odd, but it felt nice for once, not to be thought of as a liability.

Chaz looked saddened at the competition. If he'd shifted into his feline form, his tail would have been drooping. "You could use a Paladin, though, right? I'll have all sorts of different connections."

No one answered.

"Okay, I'll check back with you in a few days."

"You do that," Zeke said and followed Chaz to the door. As soon as he stepped through and turned to wave bye, the metal door slammed in his face.

TWENTY-FOUR

Zeke eyed Den who still stared at the door, his hand rubbing his chin.

"The ring," Den said. "Now there's a possibility for some quick money to up your rankings."

"Don't tell me you're thinking of doing it." Zeke accused. "There's a good chance *you know who* will be there. That's where they go to slum."

"Chaz has a point. Two of you would mean twice the chances of winning."

Kira couldn't follow their thread of conversation. Doing what?

Zeke looked over at her, his eyes alit with fire.

Kira shivered from the intensity of his gaze.

"You can't enter Kira."

What was he doing? Zeke was bargaining for her so she wouldn't die in an event? Just hours ago, she could have escaped, and he wouldn't let her. It was a bit endearing of him to speak up for her, but she didn't need someone to fight her battles.

"That's not your call," Den snapped. "It's hers."

"It is now." Zeke said.

"What's wrong with you? Don't tell me you're getting attached to a human. Think about what they did to your sister."

"That has nothing to do with this."

"It has everything to do with this. Don't be a fool like her," Den growled.

The air was packed with suffocating tension. Zeke looked like he could hurt Den at the moment.

And Zeke had a sister? But then, really, what did she know about any of them? Nothing.

And they knew nothing about her.

"Fine," Den growled. "I won't enter her for now. But you can't coddle the girl. She needs to do her part if she wants to stay here. Remember, she can't go home. Ever.

"Fine." Zeke answered.

Both guys looked at her. Clearly the truce was only temporary.

They spent the morning bringing supplies into the silo. Den had gotten a whole cart full—weapons, wood, pots and pans. She found matches, so she cleaned the old ashes out of the wood stove and found enough broken pieces of wood to get a fire going. Maybe she could cook something for them. She picked up the can of food Zeke had tossed at her earlier but couldn't find a can opener. So maybe banging the can on a rock would work.

Zeke stopped her noisy assault and took the can. With a crunch and a flick of his wrist, his fingers ripped right through the top, and he pulled the lid back. "Sorry, we have no use for can openers."

"Yeah, I guess not." She took the mangled can and dumped the contents into the pot. The can had long ago lost its label, but it looked like it was chili. She hoped it was chili. It was hard to tell. But after a few minutes of cooking, it was warm enough to eat.

Den was eating jerky out of his pack. Kira offered some to him, but he waved it off. "No, it's fine. You eat it."

She looked at Zeke and offered him some food. "Hungry?"

He looked into her pot and then deep into her eyes. "Yes, but not for that." His eyes flashed again and she took a step back.

Zeke looked conflicted at her reaction. He swallowed and headed for the door. "I'll be back." He didn't open it so much as blast through it. The door swung shut behind him with a bang.

"Should you go after him?" Kira asked when Den didn't move from the crate.

"Why?"

"Aren't you scared he's going to run away?"

Den looked at the door and then back to Kira. "Nope, not when I have what he craves most." He took another bite of his jerky and chewed it in silence, staring at her with a satisfied smile. That smile chilled her. Was she leverage against Zeke?

"When do we start training again?"

"Not worth my time. Unless…" He looked at the door Zeke had gone through and then back to her. "You get him to let you fight, and I'll train you again." He closed the bag of jerky and went to crawl into his own hammock.

She took the pot and a spoon and crawled up the ladder to eat her meal on the floor of her "room," watching Den from afar—with uncertainty.

Twenty-Five

Den and Kira had unpacked most of the goods and the various weapons, and they set them up near the door in the space Den claimed as his.

They didn't talk much. In her mind she had gone back to calling him Butt-Chin.

Zeke returned later that day with more color in his cheeks, less wild in the eyes. There were dark spots on his jacket, and Kira tried not to think about whose they were. Where he went or what he ate wasn't really her business, but honestly? As much as she wanted it not to bother her, it did. What did he prefer if human wasn't available?

When he came over, she shot him a hurt look, quickly went up the ladder, and retreated to her hammock. She refused to speak to him. It was more out of jealousy at his freedom than anything else he did. She felt trapped here, and if she couldn't make it to the surface, she wanted to help Zeke with his goal, whatever it was. If Den thought they had better chances of fighting together, she wanted to do that. But they didn't trust her out by herself, so she was under house arrest.

How was it okay for Zeke to forbid her from fighting but demand that she be part of their team? She'd just have to find a way to make him see the light. Kira smiled to herself at her new outlook. She'd have to prove that she *was* a part of the team.

And that meant fighting.

She knew that Den wouldn't train her unless Zeke would agree to her fighting, but—wow—did he spend time on Zeke. They trained and drilled most of the day and most nights went to the fights. Sometimes they didn't come back until the next morning, worn out and tired and bloodied.

And of course, when they left, Den locked her inside the silo. He said 'for her own protection,' but she knew it probably had to do with her one failed escape attempt. She had tried to find a way to climb through the hole in the ceiling but couldn't reach. She didn't have that sort of agility.

Finally, Den left—alone—to go to Ferb's and watch the big match up on TV. It was time to start placing bets. Zeke was sitting on the floor with a battered book. It was oddly comforting to see him reading. Such a human thing to do.

"Why hasn't he continued to train me?" She wanted to see what Zeke would say.

"Maybe because he's mad at me, because I won't let him enter you in the ring." He didn't even look up from his page when he answered.

So he knew. "Then let me fight."

"I have to fight in order to keep the money coming. We need food and supplies." Zeke turned a page. "You don't need to fight. You shouldn't fight—you're human."

"Gah! This is all my fault. If other humans are fighting—dying—I should be too."

"No, this isn't anyone's fault. It's just the way it is."

"Well, I hate being cooped up here, I need to do something. To train." She stood up abruptly demanded, "Train me."

"What? No!" He finally put the book down and gave her his full attention. Now that she had it, she wasn't about to let it get away. She bent down, grabbed his hands, and pulled him to his feet.

"Show me what you do in the ring. Where do you go each night?"

"No!" he pulled away and gave her his back. "It's not pretty. You don't want to know what I have to do to survive."

"I survived the gauntlet. What if I get entered in another event and I'm not prepared?"

"I'm not your sponsor or owner or trainer." He turned away, his eyes sad.

"But you care about whether I die. I don't want to die. So teach me to survive. What if you're not here to protect me next time?"

Zeke stared at her.

"Fine."

She jump around but she held it in, played it cool. She was doing something—anything—besides sitting around staring at the ceiling and sweeping the always dusty floor. This was action, this was getting her moving. This felt like she was accomplishing something.

"The ring. It's a match. Two enter and one leaves alive."

"I think we have something like that back home."

He shook his head. "Not exactly. This one is a bit rougher. You've already seen one bout."

"I have?"

"At the Gamblers' Market. You saw a version of the ring."

"Oh, I see."

Zeke moved around the room and started pushing things out of the way. "If you were entered, you can bet it wouldn't be against someone weak. Everyone would want to tear you apart. Especially after seeing you kill a boggart. There's only one kind of creature designed to kill a boggart, but you—it was a good moment for you." He smiled and drew a line in the dirt floor, motioned for Kira to stand on it.

"How many have you fought?" The outcome suddenly felt less certain.

"I've been doing it awhile." Evasive.

Zeke placed another mark on the floor, pulled a crate to the center of the room, and set a stick on it.

"Ever been injured doing it?"

He nodded. "Lots of times."

"But you always survive." She tried to sound encouraging, but…how could zombie fighting be considered fair?

He laughed. "Of course, I'm not your average zeke or half-lifer. I am a lot harder to kill." He pointed to the stove where he had set up an old alarm clock with a bell. "You ready? You never know what weapon will be provided—sometimes it's a knife, others an axe, once it was a spoon. The object is to get to it first."

"Yeah, I know it." Kira jumped up and down and shook out her arms before settling in and getting ready to run toward the crate. "It's a lot like dodgeball. Get to the ball in the middle first and then hit your opponent."

"Except you can die."

"Yeah, I'm not going to let that happen." She dug her boot into the ground and focused on the crate. She'd have to get there before him, outsmart the zombie.

"Good."

She didn't look at the clock, just listened to the ticking as the second hand moved around. Breathe in. Release. Focus.

Ring!

She was off like a bullet, racing toward the crate.

Zeke had already beaten her and picked up the stick. He held it above her head. "Too slow. You're dead."

"That's not fair. You don't know that I'd be dead already."

Zeke placed the stick back on the crate and gave her a stern look. "Yes you would. If you were playing against me you'd be. I'm faster and stronger than you."

Kira gritted her teeth and growled. "Again!" She marched back to her starting point and turned to face the crate.

Zeke reset the timer. He walked slowly back to his mark on the line. Kira could feel her anger rising. This wasn't fair. How was she supposed to outrun him? She didn't have much time to think before the bell went off again, and she shot from her mark, racing toward the crate.

Zeke got there first again.

"Gah!" She picked up the crate and tossed it at him. Zeke's eyes went wide as he ducked. The crate crashed. Pieces flew across the floor and one hit her foot.

"Nice, that's a good move. You have to assess your opponent and find their weakness. Use whatever you have available to distract them."

"Again," Kira huffed. She was lightly out of breath.

"You can't beat me, Kira." He sounded a little smug.

"I said again."

He took the broken crate and set it back in the middle of the room. Placed the stick back in the middle. "You don't get three chances in real life, Kira." He reset the clock on the stove and went to his mark.

That final taunt pushed her over the edge. Zeke was right. She'd have to assess her enemy and use his weakness. What was a zombie's weakness?

Oh. Something told her not to be so foolish—but she just couldn't make herself care. Kira turned around on her mark, giving Zeke her back. She leaned down to her boot and slipped out her knife, then picked up a piece of splintered wood in her other hand, careful to hide what she was doing. She stood back up and watched the clock. When the timer was about to go off, she turned her back to Zeke again, carefully pressed the knife into her collarbone, and made a long scratch. It started to bleed.

She grimaced but kept her focus on Zeke's reaction.

"Kira," his voice had deepened into a groan. "Please tell me you didn't." She could hear the desire in his voice and knew his eyes were probably flashing as he tried to control his hunger. "What have you done?"

The alarm rang. Kira spun and raced for the crate. Zeke had backed away from her, pressing himself against the far wall. His breathing had picked up as he tried to suppress his desire.

This time she grabbed the stake. She was smart enough to beat him.

Zeke's eyes were indeed flashing. He grinned evilly. "Good, the first part of the lesson is gaining the weapon." His eyes were locked on the blood dripping down her collarbone. His chest heaved and his head bobbed as if to a drumbeat. There was something weird about it. But familiar.

Zeke's fingers flexed and went to his side. His body tensed.

All of a sudden it hit her.

Zeke circled her. "The second part of the lesson is killing your opponent."

His head was bobbing to the rhythm of her heart.

He lunged.

TWENTY-SIX

Zeke's body hit her full force, sending both of them flying through the air. She screamed and hit the ground. Her head smacked the cement. She saw stars.

Zeke's body landed on top of her. Any second, his teeth would gnash, and he'd rip out her throat. She whimpered and turned her head.

But nothing happened. She could feel his body pressed against hers, hear his breathing rasping against her ear, but she was still alive.

He whispered, sending currents of electricity and fear through her. "What you did was very, very stupid."

She turned so she could see him, furious. "It wasn't."

Zeke shook, struggled to control himself. "I could have killed you."

"And I you." Kira smiled. She flexed her wrist and nudged him with the stick, making him feel the weapon over his heart.

"Being stabbed in the heart wouldn't stop me," he chuckled.

"No, but being stabbed through the brain would."

He froze when the knife she had hidden in her boot touched the base of his neck. "I do believe this is the right angle."

Zeke laughed again, deep and throaty. He slowly lifted himself off her. "How did you know I wouldn't lose control and kill you? I could have, you know. And why did you change the direction of the stake?"

"I don't know, I just did." She slid the knife back into her boot. Her head throbbed from the impact with the cement floor.

Zeke reached down and helped her up. Too fast. Her head swam and the room started to spin. He caught her, wrapped both of his arms around her to steady her.

She held on. Kira probably should have pulled away once the room stopped spinning, but she didn't. She didn't know what possessed her to stay in his arms, but she wasn't in a hurry to leave. Maybe she craved human contact, the warm embrace of a hug. Of course, this was absolutely settling for a zombie hug and a lukewarm embrace.

But he didn't seem to be in a hurry to release her either. In fact, he pulled her a little closer and nuzzled the top of her head.

"Don't test my restraint again." Zeke released her and stepped away. "You may think you trust me, but don't."

He turned and ran across the room. The loss of him stung like rejection.

In one long leap, he jumped ten feet up the ladder and over to the second beams. Up the next rope onto the floor he'd claimed for himself.

So much distance between them.

The silo door opened and Den entered.

Den's eyes took in the destroyed crate and bounced to Kira's bloodied shirt. He pursed his lips but didn't say anything at her injury. Instead, he lifted an eyebrow and scanned for Zeke. "Tomorrow's the big day, my boy. I've already placed my bets, and I think we're going to win big. I can feel it."

Twenty-Seven

This time when Den and Zeke got ready to leave for the night, he didn't lock her in the silo. "Come with us, Kira. Let's have some fun."

Zeke's head snapped up, and he studied Den with a worried expression, but he didn't say anything.

Kira slowly came down the ladder and stood next to Zeke. She looked at him, but he refused to make eye contact. Something was off. He knew something. Still, she didn't want to question Den's change of heart, because she needed a change of scenery, even if there wasn't much to look at underground. Out and in the city was *something.*

Zeke led the way, his hands shoved into his jacket pocket, footsteps heavier—angrier—than usual. Kira tried to keep up, but his much longer legs outpaced hers. She settled for keeping him in sight. Den was preoccupied checking the numbers on his owner's chip. He seemed a little too happy, too content. That worried her.

The ring events took place in an old club called Pandora. Loud music blasted inside, and Zeke stopped in front of the door, banging loudly. The door squealed as it rolled to the side, and he was allowed to enter. Den came up behind with Kira, and the bouncer stopped them.

He leaned down and sniffed Kira's hair. "Human."

"Mine," Zeke answered. "Insurance."

Kira tried to keep her face neutral, but she wanted to punch him. Whatever it took to get her out and about and not locked away.

"You have to pay extra to get it in." The guard wouldn't budge.

"Do you recognize this human?" Den answered roughly.

"They all look the same to me. How can I tell them apart?"

"It's the one that survived the gauntlet," Den said in the guard's ear.

"Oh really? Proceed."

Den gave her a poke that sent her scurrying into the crowd. "Now remember, you can't leave here. The doors are guarded. Besides, I know you want to see Zeke fight, right?"

"No." Her face warmed.

"Liar." Den just smiled and motioned to the dance floor where Zeke had passed through. She had lost him in the crowd of gyrating bodies. "Enjoy yourself, the fights start soon."

She'd gladly enjoy the freedom—and search for a real exit while she was at it. Moving away from Den, she hugged the walls, deeper into the warehouse. She found a bar area and thought about sneaking behind the counter and into the back room.

Her brace beeped. She looked down and read green words.

DON'T THINK ABOUT RUNNING!

What in the world? She had no idea that messages could be sent across it, let alone English. She played with the buttons and tried to adjust the settings, but it was useless. She'd love to send irritating messages to Den—or Chaz even. She'd have to have to ask Zeke to teach her, but then she didn't think he'd show her how to contact anyone, especially Chaz.

"Can I get you something to drink?" a minotaur asked from behind the bar. Kira looked at her band and realized she didn't have any tokens.

"How about a water?"

"That'll be ten tokens." He held up a remote and reached across the bar toward her band. She withdrew her arm, not wanting to show that she had zero freedom tokens.

"Really? For water?"

"Yeah, it's not free, honey. If you want free, then it's bile you get." He reached beneath the counter, and went to the faucet. A murky brown goo filled the glass. He set it on the counter with a thud and pushed it towards her. The tang of old rust hit her nose.

"Gee, thanks." Kira took the stein and carried it away from the bar. She couldn't possibly drink this, but she didn't want to upset the minotaur. She couldn't help but hold the glass a good foot in front of her. As soon as she was out of sight she placed it on a table. It was quickly picked up by an octopus monster who splashed its contents all over its head. The same octopus tried to wrap a wet tentacle around her shoulders.

She knocked off the offending arm and retreated into a dark corner. From there, she had a decent view to watch as odd groups and couples mixed and mingled at the tables—and even the dance floor.

Why not? Music and parties were a part of her world. It wasn't totally weird that monsters enjoyed music and dancing too. Although the music had a different vibe and tended to lean to the minor keys, it did have a good rhythm. She began to relax, her finger tapping the wall to the beat.

Someone with a hint of aftershave came up next to her. It was so odd to smell something so clean and fresh that she couldn't help but look up into the very handsome face of a guy a few years older than her. He had nice, even teeth, bright blue eyes, and his hair was a chestnut brown.

"Hey," he grinned her direction and glanced away, a little bashful.

Kira was totally taken with him. She laughed. "Hi." Did she just giggle? Oh, she wanted to kill herself for sounding so juvenile.

"I'm Olivier." He held out his pale hand, and she shook it.

"Kira." His hand felt warm to the touch.

"You look familiar, Kira. Have you been here before?"

"Um, no. First time."

"It's so odd. I swear I've met you."

"No, I'm pretty sure I'd remember if I'd met you." There it went. That stupid giggle again. Her cheeks burned in embarrassment.

"Do you want to dance?" Olivier held his hand out to her. She wasn't a good dancer, but she so wanted to be near him.

He pulled her into the throng at the center of the dance. It took a few moments for her fear to fade—the scaly beast thrashing next to her could totally rip her to shreds—but it did. She was just dancing. She closed her eyes and focused on the music. When she opened them again, the monsters had faded into the background.

Only Olivier mattered in that moment.

"You have the most beautiful eyes." He had to lean down to give her the compliment, yelling in her ear to be heard over the music.

She threw her head back and laughed. "Thanks."

She felt someone watching her—was that Zeke?—and she hesitated for a moment. No, she shoved her concern aside. Why should she feel guilty dancing with someone else? It wasn't like *he* had asked her to dance. She spotted Zeke against a wall and thought she saw his head shake.

What was his problem? Now he was bossing her around. He wasn't Den. If he wanted her to stop dancing, he'd better get over here and tell her to her face. She turned her back on him and focused on Olivier again. At least this was someone who seemed happy to be with her. She glanced only once more over her shoulder.

Zeke wasn't there. Not her problem anymore.

It felt so good to let loose and be free on the dance floor. She didn't worry about Den or Zeke. She just let herself be, feel in the moment. She wanted to live, and right now, she felt very alive.

Maybe because of the way Olivier looked at her. She couldn't tear herself away from his possessive eyes. She was drawn to him, so much that she moved closer.

He smiled in delight and rested his hands on her upper arms. A shock ran through her body at his touch, and she couldn't pull away. He whispered into her ear again. "Come with me."

This time, there was no missing his voice over the music. It hit her in her very soul. She felt her body following him to the darkened corner and into a back hall.

She wanted to tell him no. Stop. Where are we going?

Her mouth wouldn't work. He pulled her against a wall and his hand brushed against her hair. He leaned in and pressed his lips to her temple.

"Oh, Kira, you smell so sweet. I must taste you."

Her body froze, and her soul screamed *no*. He was controlling her. She didn't know how, but he was controlling her.

His mouth moved lower and he kissed her ear, then along her jaw line. Something sharp grazed her cheek.

She started to panic, but she couldn't move away. Couldn't call for help. Her mind cried out for help, but she couldn't move. A mirror across the hall played the scene like a horror flick, and she had to watch. His jaw muscle flexed and—

Sharp. Prick. He bit into her neck.

Her mouth opened. It was nothing like the movies. They lied. It wasn't pleasure to be seduced by a vampire. It was pain.

Finally, a scream escaped her mouth. A few moments later, he withdrew from her neck. She saw the blood, *her* blood, dribble from his lip.

Horrible.

Olivier lifted her hand above her head and turned her band over. She heard the sound of tokens being transferred, and he smiled softly at her. He was paying her for services rendered. How humiliating.

She never consented to what he did.

"It's been so long since I've tasted human. I look forward to another rendezvous." He smiled and she saw his vampire fangs. How foolish she was.

She couldn't move, still in his thrall. Trapped within her own mind. When he moved away, she slid down the wall and collapsed on the floor. Her neck burned like fire where he'd bitten her, and tears poured out of her eyes, but she was unable to even control her eyelids and blink them away. Her vision blurred and her soul cried out in fury.

Twenty-Eight

She saw red. A lot of it.

And it wasn't her blood. It was her fury burning.

Someone ran down the hall toward her, and then Zeke's face swam through her tears. She focused on him.

"Kira." He helped sit her up, and she was finally able to blink. The rush of tears poured down her cheek.

"Heh bith me!" The bite hurt like someone had branded her with a hot iron, and the rest of her neck felt really wet. The worst of it was that her strength still felt like it was draining.

"Let me see." He pushed her hair off of her shoulder and gasped at her wound. "He bit you too deep. He nicked something."

When he pulled away from her, his eyes flashed in hunger. "You need a doctor, fast."

She tried to stand but almost immediately started to fall. As Zeke caught her, his cool mouth brushed her bleeding neck. He shoved her body against the wall and snapped his head away, his arms like iron as he held her there immobile. Kept her at a distance. He wouldn't even look at her.

A smear of blood remained on his mouth, and he shook his head, trying to focus. His body quivered.

"Zeke. Make the pain stop."

His body trembled at her request. "Kira." He exhaled her name and it came out like a growl. "I can help you, but you'll hate me after."

She looked into his deep brown eyes, knew it would be impossible to hate him. "Please." She didn't even know what she was asking. She just knew that she trusted him.

Zeke dropped his arms and crushed his body to hers. He pressed his lips to hers and kissed her—hard enough to bruise her lips. His desire rushed through her, but then he softened against her.

She answered his kiss with her own. Matched him with emotion. He pulled away from her, his eyes now flashing with power. He reached down and pulled the knife out of her boot. Pressed the handle it into her right hand.

"Just in case," he said. His lips brushed hers with another kiss, and then he ducked to press his mouth to her wound.

Where the vampire's kiss burned with pain, the zombie's kiss bathed her with warmth. Her skin stretched and her muscles pulled as they slowly healed. She felt strong, invincible and exhilarated. She wrapped her arms around Zeke to pull him closer, but he yanked himself out of her arms and flung himself across the room.

Blood, his blood had made a trail on her shirt. He'd nicked himself on her knife. His eyes were flashing white, and he was panting. Kira watched the mirror across the hall—her neck healed before her eyes. Zombies had regenerative abilities, but she'd never imagined he could heal her with his own kiss. Was it because he tasted her blood?

Zeke had curled up into a ball, groaning like he was in pain. "Zeke," She ran to him.

"Go away before I do much worse to you than the vampire."

"No, I won't leave you." She kneeled next to him and lifted his head, so that his flashing eyes stared directly into her soul. "You saved my life. I owe you."

"I didn't save it just to take it from you," he whispered. "I needed your blood to heal you. Healing makes me hungry. I need to feed and you're too close."

"Oh!" Of course he did. Here she was tempting him with herself.

"Go! Go away. Please, I'll find you later, but leave me before I do something I regret."

She wanted to, she did. But she couldn't just leave him there in such misery.

"Go AWAY!" Zeke growled and pushed her away so hard she flew backwards and hit the wall.

Her back hurt. She looked up at Zeke's horrified expression.

She was furious—but not at him. She was angry at herself, for what she had let herself get duped into. She wanted revenge and, right now, with Zeke's healing ability flowing through her, she felt like she could take on the world.

Even a vampire.

Heck, that's what they were here for. A fight. Well, she was going to give it to them.

Ready to destroy Olivier, she turned back out toward the large room. Whoa. While she was under the vampire's thrall and then healing, the room had been transformed. She'd had no idea.

The music was still just as loud, but now the DJ was announcing the fights. A keg had been placed in the middle of the dance floor. No one stepped onto the wooden square, but bodies were pressed almost up to the edges.

She stayed on the outskirts and watched as the first challenger stepped into the makeshift ring. A man with a mohawk, a leather vest, and black pants raised his arms, and a cheer came from the crowd. He strutted around the floor, taunting challengers. Whenever he leaned back, a plume of fire and smoke blasted from his mouth. She watched as his skin rippled—scales underneath.

Dragon.

His challenger was a man whose metal skin reflected the lights, creating a liquid metal look. Kira watched the huge wall-mounted TV screens light up with bets as people made wagers from their bands. Den's name appeared at the top of the screen. He'd placed a large sum of money on the dragon.

A bright orb floated down from the rafters and a spear appeared on the keg. Whoa. Who had the power to conjure items? This event had a different feel than the others. More personal.

And perfect for getting revenge.

Kira stalked the floor, hunting her prey. Beside her, the battle ensued between the dragon and metal man. She couldn't help but think of a knight fighting a dragon. Legends had been born from this kind of epic battle, and it was now worthy of a mere bar brawl. Maybe because it was always obvious that the knight would win.

"Boo!" The monster next to her yelled, and she heard the two fighters clash. The dragon roared in pain.

"Finish him!" another called out.

She moved on, walking on her toes to catch a glimpse of Olivier.

An uncontrolled blast of fire spewed across the crowd a mere foot from where Kira had just stood. Her back warm, she turned and saw that nothing but ash remained of the loud bystander who'd taunted the dragon.

By now, fear would have kicked in to a normal girl, but Kira realized in that moment, she'd never been like most girls. Didn't care about hair or clothes. She cared about honor and respect, and both of those had been stolen from her tonight.

There he was. Olivier watched the ongoing battle with delight. His eyes burned red with power, probably because he had just fed…on her.

A loud, anguished roar filled the air, quickly drowned out by the loud cheers of the winners and the hiss of the losers.

The ring was cleared, and another challenger was called the floor. She hadn't even seen who won.

Olivier strutted onto the floor, and she heard a collective boo from the crowd. Not a crowd favorite then.

The werewolf next to her started to growl, and he moved forward to challenge the vampire. Kira grabbed his arm. Powerful muscle ripple through his arm—he almost shook her off. He snapped at her, but she pulled at her bloody shoulder to show him the scar on her neck.

"I have unfinished business with the vamp. Do you mind?"

The werewolf eyed her, surprised. "He'll just mind roll you again." He gave her a cursory sniff and paused, his hackles rising. "I smell blood. Hmm…not yours…dead man's blood." He touched the still-wet trail of Zeke's blood on her shirt.

"If I fail, then you can have your chance after me."

He nodded.

Kira rushed onto the floor and felt a moment of satisfaction to see Olivier's shocked expression.

A hush fell over the room.

"You. You want to challenge me?" He put his hand over his stomach and laughed. "Come on, you stand no chance. I rolled you like a ball down a hill."

"You took something from me without my permission."

"Oh really? Most love a vampire's kiss." He held out his hands to try and entice the crowd.

They remained silent.

"I've had better. In fact, one just a few minutes ago put yours to shame."

The room burst into laughter, and Olivier's eyes glowed red.

"I will make you pay!" He yelled, pointing his finger at her.

She held up her band. "You're kidding. You're not worth it. Here, do you want your money back?"

Olivier looked up toward the ceiling and yelled, "Challenge accepted."

Kira followed his gaze. A darkened balcony hid observers in the shadows. She couldn't focus on them with the spotlights aimed at her, so she drew her attention back to the keg. Waited to see what would drop on the table for a weapon.

An orb drifted down from above, probably from the watchers' balcony, and alit on the keg. The light dissipated.

In the middle of the keg lay a silver cross.

Olivier's face went white. His head snapped up. "Oh, come on! Now's not the time to have a sense of humor, Hermes."

No response came from the darkness.

Kira smiled. "I think someone wants you dead…oh wait. That's me." She couldn't believe her luck. A vampire couldn't touch a cross.

Zeke had told her to study her opponent and use his own weakness against him. What else did she know about vampire lore? She scoured her mind. Hollywood got so many things wrong, but Ferb had mentioned one thing most movies got right—weapons that can harm monsters.

"Get in line, precious." Olivier spoke, and they both moved to their chalk marks on the floor. "Never mind if I can't touch it. I'll just kill you with my bare hands. Or my teeth." He ran his tongue across his fangs.

Disgusted, Kira glanced up at the screen and saw that Den had just wagered on the fight. Oh. He'd bet a lot of money that she'd lose.

Not only lose—that she'd be killed.

She spun around the room, searching for Den. How dare he assume she'd just die, she was a fighter? He should have some faith in her. She wanted to wring his neck. Zeke pushed through the crowd, his face looked white in horror. He shook his head and motioned for her to come off the floor.

She mouthed the word *no* and looked up at the screen. The countdown had begun.

Zeke moved so he was in her line of site and motioned again, this time to her neck.

She nodded and reached up to touch the blood still making her shirt sticky. She smeared it on her hand and watched as Olivier's nostrils flared.

"That won't work on me. I've already fed."

The alarm rang, and she raced toward the silver cross. She held it firm, as Olivier paced the outside of the ring. His fangs and fingers had elongated. He tried to swipe at her but missed. She smeared the end of the cross with blood from her shirt.

"What, you think the scent of your blood is so tempting I'll just throw myself onto the cross? You weren't that great of a thrall."

"Oh, stop with the talking and just fight already. What, are you scared of a puny human girl you bragged about rolling so easily?"

Olivier hissed and came at her. One second he was in front, the next he disappeared in a black cloud. Something grabbed her from behind and tossed her across the ring. She landed hard on the floor and slid into the crowd.

A clawed hand picked her back up and set her on her feet. She met the gray werewolf's eyes. "You can do it!" he encouraged. And he gave her a push back toward the ring. She had lost the cross.

Olivier appeared in front of her again and, with another push, sent her flying across the room. She opened her eyes to see the metal wall coming at an amazing speed. She hit it so hard that she dented it. She slid to the ground and groaned. What would that have done to her without Zeke's power running through her?

Olivier's shiny black loafers walked slowly to her.

Something glinted not too far off, along the floor. The cross.

"See, I told you you wouldn't stand a chance against me." His shoes did a little dance along the floor near her head.

She kept her eyes on the cross. Her fingers moved. The werewolf moved to the cross. She met the beast's eyes. A look of understanding passed between them, and he nodded.

"I don't just stand against you," she whispered.

Olivier bent closer. "Speak up, girl. You're too weak for everyone to hear."

"I stand against everything you are. I will not let you take advantage of anyone else, ever again."

"Why won't you just die?"

"'Cause that wouldn't make a very good movie, now would it?" Kira held out her hand toward the werewolf.

The werewolf grimaced in pain as his skin touched the silver, but he slid the cross across the floor to her. Kira picked up the cross and stabbed it into Olivier's chest.

Olivier staggered back, staring at the silver protruding from his chest. He tried to remove the cross, but every time his hand touched it, it burned him. "Impossible." He howled in pain and fell to his knees. Gasping for breath, his red eyes lost their brilliance. And power. His pale skin turned even whiter, and he started to fade away. "How did you do it?"

"I poisoned you."

"But how?"

"Dead man's blood"—Kira touched her shirt stained with Zeke's blood—"is poison to vampires."

He fell to the ground, and the room started to cheer. Kira leaned over him as he cried out in pain.

"Say you're sorry."

"What?"

"Say you're sorry and that you'll never do what you did to me again without someone's permission. Or I'll leave it in."

Olivier squealed like a frightened little girl. All of a sudden, he didn't seem very attractive anymore.

"I'm sorry, I'm sorry. I'm sooorrrryy! Please, help me."

"Also say that you concede. 'Cause I'd rather not kill you."

"Okay, ah…ah. It hurts. You win." He bawled and the room booed.

Kira leaned down, pulled the cross out of Olivier's chest, flung it across the floor. The crowd erupted into cheers and howls. She turned and found Zeke standing against a far wall. His eyes weren't flashing anymore. He looked proud of her.

Den on the other hand looked furious.

A large clawed hand touched her shoulder, and Kira looked up into the werewolf's face. She gently took the werewolf's hand and turned it over. The ugly burn on his palm made her want to cry. "I'm forever grateful for your help."

"And I yours."

"What do you mean?"

"I was in the white drop tube with you in the gauntlet. You could have left us, but you stayed to help. I just returned the favor."

"I…I…" Never had she expected that kind of honor and loyalty. "Thank you."

"We're even." He pulled his hand away hid his injury. "I don't like being in debt."

"Neither do I," Kira said. "What's your name?"

"Howl." He looked away uncomfortably, and a murmur around them began to grow louder. The werewolf was a head taller than everyone else. Whatever he saw made him quickly pull away. "Run," he whispered before he turned and shifted into human form.

Kira only saw the back of his head and a gray scruff of hair.

Zeke appeared next to her and grabbed her hand. "Come on, Kira. They've noticed you, which is very, very bad."

"Who has?" She looked around, and saw Den look at his band. He seemed about to cry.

"Follow me." Zeke pulled her roughly through the throng of people and started to run for the door.

A blinding light enveloped them and she couldn't see.

Those closest to her cried out in fright, and she covered her eyes with her forearm.

"Leaving so soon?" A silky voice called out to her from the light.

Twenty-Nine

When the light faded, a giant spot that radiated from a strange being kept her blinded. The light blocked her exit. She tried to see around whoever it was but couldn't.

She stood, alone, in the middle of the room. Zeke was gone. The crowd had moved to the far corners and watched, frozen in fear.

"Impressive." The sparkling man clapped his hands slowly as the light faded so she could see him. An exaggerated clap meant to draw attention his way. "For one so young. Don't you agree, Ares?"

"And one so mortal, Hermes" Ares replied. His hand came up to stroke his chin, and Kira noticed he wore four silver rings, each with an emblem of a horse. He looked so normal for a myth. Ares could have been the lead singer for a rock band. He wore his long dark hair pulled into a man bun, black clothes, and jeans tucked into black boots.

Hermes, on the other hand, was slim of frame and face, his hair immaculately combed over in a gentlemen's cut. His smile came too freely, probably bestowed many times a day. He wore white pants and a pale pink shirt that made his cheeks seem flushed, as if he was holding onto a secret he couldn't tell. She guessed, since he was the messenger, he'd probably heard many secrets and gossip over the years. The look was probably suiting.

Den watched her, standing within the onlookers. His expression said he was not pleased.

"How ever did you get down here"—Hermes waved his hands in a circle—"into our world?"

She looked at Den, and he shook his head. What was she not supposed to say? That she'd been stolen from the surface by Alpo and Vic? There were so many things wrong with how she had even gotten here, she thought for sure they'd at least hear her plea.

Maybe let her go home.

"Someone stole me from above and sold me on the slave market." There. It was the truth, but she hadn't said any names. That couldn't possibly get her in trouble.

"I see. How very troubling." Hermes feigned an expression of concern as Ares approached her.

She felt small under his gaze.

He noticed her arm band and lifted it up to look at the tokens and the brand of the eagle. "Look, Hermes. This is the human that survived the gauntlet...the one that's been avoiding our summons."

"Oh, how magnificent. I think we need to have her." Hermes looked around the crowd and waited for someone to step forward and claim her.

Kira craned her neck, frustrated that she didn't see Zeke anywhere. Had he run away? Den came forward, and Hermes waved his arm, bringing him into their circle.

He glanced down at Den's band. "Oh, too bad. You wagered poorly on her and lost. We can help you with that and take her off your hands," Hermes stated.

Den looked uneasy, sweat dripping of off his brow. "Uh no, I'd like to keep her. For my zeke, you see?" He swiped his hand outward and turned to see that he was in the room alone.

"I don't see any zeke." Ares's voice boomed with authority. "You know the penalty for bringing a human down here. It's obvious she didn't come from a human farm in the borderlands."

"I didn't bring her here."

"That's not what Nessie said," Hermes laughed. "She reported that you and two others brought her here in the canals. See, we hate being lied to."

"He's not lying," Kira spoke up. "Alpo and Vic took me from my home, and Remus bought me at the Gamblers' Market. Den saved me from being fed to a zeke."

Ares's eyes turned so dark in color that it was hard to distinguish where the pupil and iris ended. "Did he really? Or did you save yourself? Think about what you just said."

Kira paused and tried to rethink everything that had happened. Yes, she was the one who saved herself from Creeper. Was Ares a human lie detector? It sure sounded like he could hear the half-truths.

What was she supposed to do when the makers of the games themselves were confronting her? Maybe the safest action was to stay quiet. Besides, they seemed to know everything about her, even when she lied.

"We've decided to relieve you of your human companion." Hermes smiled and waved his finger in the direction of Den's arm band. Kira could hear the sound of tokens loading as it filled. She watched as a smile played at the corner of his mouth. It must have been a large sum, because he wouldn't look at her. "Now that should buy your silence."

"I'm free," Kira stated proudly. "I don't belong to him."

"Nonsense. You have a bracer. You belong to Underland and therefore…us."

"NOOooo!" A loud, anguished cry came from somewhere in the rafters. It sounded like Zeke.

"Oh ho! Is that who I think it is?" Hermes scanned the darkness above in excitement.

"I think it is," Ares confirmed. He turned to Den, his face void of any emotion. "So he's your *zeke*," he said the word with emphasis.

Den's face turned red, but he wouldn't look away. He neither denied nor confirmed it. And that was enough for Ares.

"You tell him we're taking the girl for insurance, and he needs to stop his foolish plan—both of you." Ares called toward the roof. "You hear that?"

Den nodded and faded back into the crowd, abandoning her.

Kira stared into the darkened balcony where the Hermes and Ares had watched the match and thought she saw movement, but the lights kept her from being sure. Zeke was up there. Suddenly, a spotlight came loose from the ceiling and plummeted down toward Hermes.

Hermes snapped his fingers and disappeared as the spotlight crashed into the ground and shattered. He appeared next to it and wrinkled his nose in disdain. "Oh really, now who's going to clean up this mess?"

"If you want the human, you know what you have to do," Ares said, his voice echoing in the near empty warehouse.

"Never!" Zeke's voice carried.

"Then you shall never see her again," Ares threatened.

Another spotlight came hurtling down toward them. "Very well." Ares clutched Kira to him. A black cloud of smoke wrapped around both her and the Greek god and they disappeared, just as the spotlight crashed into the floor.

THIRTY

Kira woke up in a room surrounded by flickering candlelight and soft, downy pillows. The first thing she noticed was how pristine everything was in this round room. In a way, it felt like she was back inside the silo, except it was cleaner, smelled better.

Kira sat up in the pile of pillows and noticed she was wearing a dress of blue. A braid hung over her shoulder—they'd washed her hair! She touched her braid. Oh. Even her nails had been trimmed and polished.

While bits of it were a nice change, Kira found it disorienting to be so feminine. She felt like a part of her armor had disappeared with her boots and knife.

And the brace on her wrist.

"Where am I?" She didn't expect an answer as she looked around the glowing white room.

"Olympus Tower," a feminine voice responded behind her. Kira turned and saw a beautiful woman sitting on a chaise lounge, her hair long and auburn red, her dress a deep emerald green.

"Who are you?" Kira asked.

"Names no longer matter to me." She looked down at her hands, gently clasped in her lap.

"Of course names matter. Are you saying you don't have one?"

"I don't know. At least I cannot recall. You could give me one." She actually looked hopeful.

Kira stared at the solemn woman and could feel her pain, evident across the room. Why would this beautiful woman be denied her own name? She tried to think of a reason and it finally came to her. "You're being punished for something, aren't you? Zeke said the gods and goddesses lost some of their power because they were forgotten. Is that what happened? Did you forget who you are, or did Underland forget you?"

Her cheery complexion turned dark with anger. "Don't you dare speak to me like that, you mortal fool!" She jumped up and her hand came forward to point in Kira's direction, but nothing happened. No power, flash of light, or spark.

Kira was right. She was powerless. It seemed that she had some sort of intuition of who or what she was supposed to be, but she couldn't remember.

"Why am I here?" Kira asked the forgotten goddess.

"It seems that someone thinks you are special. You've caught their attention, so you are bidden to be here for the time being."

"I don't believe in mythical gods," Kira said firmly.

"Careful what you say aloud here. That can be a death sentence."

"Death doesn't scare me," Kira lied.

"You'd be foolish to not fear Death, for I've met him. He is quite frightening." The woman beckoned with her head toward the door. "Come, I have something to show you."

A door appeared out of the rock, and Kira followed the nameless goddess into the hallway. They walked down a spiral staircase, into another hall, and through a set of golden doors. This room looked like a museum. Large white columns, tables with vases and cups, tapestries hung on the wall. Three women sat in the center weaving on a giant loom.

The woman led her over and had Kira take a look at their work.

There was something wrong with the tapestry they were weaving. Even though the three women were using spools of brightly colored thread, half of the tapestry had turned black.

"This is what our world has been reduced to," the nameless goddess said. "Once, long ago, the tapestry was whole and not divided between dark and light. Now, our world has been split asunder. The tapestry only shows us the future of our realm, the Underland. The Fates cannot control what happens on your world any more than the gods below can. But these women, the Fates, they can see it. They weave it, but it is not for our eyes. The darkness is spreading and we Underlanders are dying. And there is nothing we can do to stop it."

"There must be something," Kira said.

"Look, Kira Lier, and tell me what you see."

Kira walked over to the loom. She stared at the blackened half of the tapestry, trying to see what had once been displayed. Nothing was there but black thread. Over and over, the woman pushed the shuttle with gold wool through the loom and it turned slowly black.

Whatever picture she was weaving would disappear.

Kira leaned closer to the woman nearest the black part of the loom. She stared, concentrated. Suddenly, the darkness parted, and Kira could see color underneath.

It looked like an alley—one in the pearl district that she was familiar with. She leaned a little closer and saw a box next to a dumpster, a girl that looked like her. It was her world.

Not just her world, but her.

The Fate whose weaving turned black, her face hidden by a shawl, picked up a pair of scissors and cut off a loose piece of thread. She started to hum off-key, and Kira recognized the tune. The woman rocked and sang under her breath, "Kira Lier brings death wherever she goes."

"It can't be," Kira breathed out in fear. But one look at the ringed fingers, thick as sausages said it must be. Kira's hand shook as she reached up to touch the woman's arm. The woman turned her head, and Kira saw her face beneath the head shawl. She jumped.

Madame Fortuna sat before her. Her eyes white as death and unseeing, she continued to push the shuttle through the loom, cut the cord, and sing softly to herself.

"So it's true then," the nameless goddess said softly. "You *can* see the dark side of the tapestry?" Her hands brushed the darkened, finished section, and she looked up at Kira hopefully. "What about her? You've seen her before…in your world maybe?" She pointed to Madame Fortuna.

"Yeah." Kira felt her patience suddenly departing. "She's just a kooky old fortune teller. She spoke my name and death, lots of death."

"No, this is Atropos, one of the Fates. She must have been trying to send you a message in your world."

"I wish I could have heeded it too, and never showed up here."

The goddess pursed her lips and spun her hair around her finger. "I think you must go. You can't stay here. Hermes and Ares must think you're their champion."

"I don't even understand who I am. I'm nobody."

"No, the reason Hermes brought the games back was because long ago, a great and terrible killer was foretold, one who would save us from the darkness. As you can see, the blackness of the loom is slowly spreading like a disease."

"The games were their way of searching for that person—to find that gruesome champion, the killer the prophecy foretold."

"I think they would have found them after thousands of years," Kira said a little frustrated.

"No, all of the champions have failed the final test. The Underlords have become desperate as more of the races here are losing power. We're forgetting ourselves. They've been sending criminals to the games for years, then the slaves, and anyone that's in debt. They've tried to raise the stakes and glorified the competitors. But no one has completed the final game. I think the Fates got it wrong. They haven't been searching for a killer. They've been searching for you...Kira Lier."

Kira's legs weakened, and her world started to spin. "You're wrong. You have to be."

"You think the gauntlet and the ring are horrible. You haven't even seen the Labyrinth." The woman looked worried. "We must get you away from here."

"Can you help me get home?" Kira asked feeling a shred of hope.

"I do not have the power to send you back home, but I know of one who can. Come." The woman left the weaving room, and Kira couldn't help but stare at the one called Atropos. Was she really the same woman who appeared to her in the alley or just a projection of her?

"Really, I can go home?" Kira asked. She felt like Dorothy at the end of the Wizard of Oz. All she had to do was click her red ruby slippers together and she could be back on the surface.

The surface.

Following the woman, she paused at an open window and looked out of Olympus Tower. So many lights were scattered for miles in the darkness. The main overhead lights were dimmed, so it must be the allotted night time. One of those lights came from the silo, where Zeke and Den were.

She pressed on, an ache in her chest.

She hadn't gotten to say goodbye. She even missed Chaz and—she hated to admit it—Warrick. Wow, now she really felt like she was reliving a book, because the thought of leaving those three really made her pause.

For once, she had friends. And she couldn't honestly call her feelings for Zeke friendly. They were something so much more. If she left, she might never see him again.

No, she definitely wouldn't ever see him again.

She'd never find her way back to Underland. Everything she'd learned here seemed impossible. Like she was reading a fairytale. Not a fairytale. A Greek myth. It was surreal.

They went down the set of spiral stairs until they ended in front of a black wooden door. "There's only one person I know of with the power to send you back to your home."

"Who is it?" Kira asked as she stared at the door. Deep scratch marks marred the wood, and she feared that this was a trap—that behind this door was another monster.

"Knock, Kira Lier, and enter," the woman spoke. "Don't be frightened. For you'll soon be home."

She stared at that door and felt a moment's hesitation. Home. Where was it going to send her—to her mother's? Back to the streets?

"Why do you hesitate?" the woman asked.

"My friends. I didn't get to say goodbye." Kira turned and felt her stomach drop. "I can't go without—"

"Listen to yourself," she scoffed. "Are you telling me you prefer living here as a slave? What kind of life is that? You are a human. You belong with your kind."

Yes, she was right. As much as she could talk herself in circles, there was no future for her here. If she stayed, she'd eventually end up dead, or eaten.

But the reality of going home felt so daunting to her. She knew, no matter where she went, it wouldn't be home. Home is where the heart is. Currently, that was down in Underland with a certain undead monster.

She really needed to figure out how to fall for normal people, someone mortal. Someone human.

The woman stepped back, and Kira reached out her hand and knocked on the black door. It opened inward and she saw nothing beyond the lighted path in the doorway. "Hello?" she called out.

Something moved beyond the door, and Kira stepped inside. Every part of her wanted to run away, but if the woman said this was the only way to go back, then she needed to speak to the man who could send her there.

"Come in," the voice echoed. It wasn't a terrifying voice. It had a pleasant tone to it, like a grandfather speaking to a child. Kira took another step inside.

The door slammed behind her, encasing her in black, nothingness. Something touched her and she felt herself falling—

Down

Down

Until she hit bottom.

The raindrops felt like ice as they touched her skin and rolled off the back of her hand.

Rain?

She shivered and opened her eyes. Blinked. She was lying on the cold wet street. The sound of a distant car horn had her covering her ears as she looked around in confusion. Where was she? She looked up and saw a brick two-story building and a light from a window.

A hiss from the sewers had Kira scrambling to her feet. Everything looked foreign, but at the same time strangely familiar. She could smell the scent of fresh baked bread. She knew exactly where she was.

She had made it back to the upper world. She was back in Portland.

THIRTY-ONE

Life had resumed. Although not much had changed since she'd come back from Underland. Madame Fortuna's shop was closed, gone out of business. Kira had gone to the post office to see if the old woman left a forwarding address. But the attendant behind the counter told her there had never been a fortune teller at that address.

Kira mostly spent her days wandering, looking for meaning. She stepped into a pub and watched the football game on TV. It felt odd. She couldn't help but look at her wrist and see the spot where her brace would have been. She pulled the sleeve of her jacket down over her bare wrist and felt as if she was missing something.

As crazy as it was, she had earned and lost more freedom tokens down below than she had ever earned surviving on her own. No, she didn't miss fighting to earn them, or almost dying. But she did miss that—for a moment—she had something. Something that was hers.

Zeke's absence was the hardest to get over. She missed him…bad. She hadn't known how much it affected her until she found herself wandering the streets, looking into the gutters. Twice she'd used a crow bar to pry up a manhole and walked around the sewers looking for the wall with the graffiti, the one that said Monsters.

Even if she found it, though, it would be impossible to find her way back. Each time, she left the sewers a little more dejected. She wandered. Slept on benches, hardly ate, and wandered again. What was she even looking for? Answers maybe?

She went back to the alley and stared at the dumpster, at the spot she had been sleeping in all those nights ago. She took a few steps back and surveyed the scene. It looked almost like the same scene in the tapestry, the one Atropos was weaving.

Kira realized she was looking at it from the wrong angle. She needed to get higher.

Kira looked over her shoulder and saw the fire escape ladder. That would do it. With a lot of pushing, she got the dumpster over to the ladder and pulled herself up on top. She leapt and caught the bottom rung, pulling the ladder down. Once she got up to the second floor, she surveyed the scene again. She still needed to go higher.

Kira climbed one more floor and looked out over the alley.

This. This was the angle the tapestry had shown her. The angle the Fate had weaved that no one could see but her.

But why? What was such a big deal about her alley? Kira turned behind her and noticed the window of the building was slightly ajar. Brown paper was taped over the dusty glass, so she couldn't see inside. She pulled up. The wooden window shuddered as it lifted.

Kira ducked and stepped inside the building.

There was just enough light from outside to illuminate a path to the middle of the room where a light bulb dangled. She reached up and pulled the chain. The room lit up, and a stone door appeared. Whoa. Totally out of place in a 1930s industrial building. The door, surrounded by sandstone, seemed thousands of years old.

There was a symbol on the door.

Kira moved to touch it.

"Kira." A voice called to her from beyond. She knew that voice.

"Zeke?" Kira turned. He stood in the empty room with her. She ran to him. "How did you find me? How did you get here to Portland?" The questions came tumbling out.

"I'm not in Portland." His arms wrapped around her, and she could feel the warmth of him. Why did he feel warm, when he'd always been cool to the touch? Something was wrong.

"What do you mean?" She pulled back and looked up at him.

He looked down and smiled, gently touching her forehead to his. "You're not in Portland either. You've never left the Underland. Hypnos has control of you. You need to wake up, Kira, before they see you found it."

"Found what? And what do you mean wake up, Zeke?" He pulled away and she felt him fade into the darkness of the room as if he was being pulled by an unseen force.

"Wake up, Kira!" He commanded. His voice grew distant.

"Zeke, I am awake!" She cried out and spun in circles, searching for him. "Don't leave me."

"I won't ever leave you, Kira. But you need to wake up and wake up NOW!" His command shook her to her very soul.

Something inside of Kira snapped.

She gasped.

And woke up.

Chanda Hahn is a New York Times and USA Today Bestselling Author. She uses experience as a children's pastor, children's librarian and bookseller to write compelling and popular fiction for teens. She was one of Amazon's top customer favorite authors of 2012 and is an ebook bestseller in five countries.

She was born in Seattle, Washington, grew up in Nebraska, and currently resides in Portland, Oregon with her husband and their twin children.

Visit Chanda Hahn's website to learn more about her other forthcoming books. www.chandahahn.com

CPSIA information can be obtained
at www.ICGtesting.com
Printed in the USA
LVOW04s1752021216
515533LV00010B/1043/P